TROUBLE BREWING

Just then ole Rod Corley come a'hustling into the Hooch House. He was one of Silver Spike's cow hands. He looked around and spied his boss and come a'running over.

"Mister Hanlon," he said. "I got to see you right away."

"Well, I'm right here, Rod," Silver Spike said. "What is it?"

Ole Rod, he looked kinda sheepish at me and then at Hooper. "It's Billy," he said.

"Well?" Silver Spike said. "What about him?"

"He's been killed, Mister Hanlon," Rod said.

Ole Silver Spike's face went kinda white, and he looked up at Rod.

"How?" he said.

Rod looked back at Hooper.

"Well, sir," he said.

"Come on," said Silver Spike. "Out with it."

"It was Davey Cline," said Rod. "One of Mister Hooper's hands. He shot him."

The Gunfighter
Robert J. Conley

LEISURE BOOKS NEW YORK CITY

A LEISURE BOOK®

February 2001

Published by

Dorchester Publishing Co., Inc.
276 Fifth Avenue
New York, NY 10001

ISBN 0-8439-4834-5

The name "Leisure Books" and the stylized "L" with design are trademarks of Dorchester Publishing Co., Inc.

Printed in the United States of America.

Visit us on the web at www.dorchesterpub.com.

The Gunfighter

Chapter One

Asininity had come once again to be a peaceable little town, and me, I come to like it thataway. You see, I was town marshal there, and while I was a-living on a reputation as a tough son of a bitch (partly on account of what that silly-ass writing fella Dingle had writ about me), one what had put away the Bensons once, and when they come outa prison had kilt them all, and one what had done in the Marlin Gang all by his lonesome, to tell you the stone truth of the matter, I was feeling just a little old and tired. I come to like it peaceable. I had my marshaling job what paid me okay, and I had my business interests what, being marshal, I had been able to create a monopoly for, and I had my Lillian and our snot-nosed little brat. I also had ole Bonnie Boodle on the side, and if Lillian knowed that for sure, why, hell, she never hardly said nothing about it.

It was the middle of the day, and I had done drunk me a pretty fair amount of good whiskey and gone on upstairs in the Hooch House to have a midday romp with ole Bonnie. We was just laying around a-taking it easy after a little spree, you know. I was kinda toying with her great floppy titties, but that was just about all. I decided that it was time to have me another drink, and I said, "Sweets, why don't you get up and pour me a little glass of that good brown whiskey?"

"Why don't you get your lazy ass up and pour it for yourself?" she said. Bonnie never had been overfull of the milk of human kindness. "I done all the work. And while you're up, pour me another one."

Well, hell, I heaved my old ass up and outa that bed and started to walk over to the table where the bottles and glasses was at, but I just happened to glance out the winder, and that was when I first seen him. I didn't know who the hell he was, but I sure as hell tuck note of him. He was a-riding a big black horse what was wearing a fancy black saddle with silver stuff decorating it all over. And he was a-wearing a black suit. It was a warm day, and he had tuck off his coat and throwed it behind him on the saddle, so he had on just the black vest and a white shirt on top. His hat was black too. And he wore two six-guns. I seen that right away, as I'm always suspicious of a man what totes two guns.

"What the hell are you doing just standing there nekkid at the winder?" Bonnie said.

"Come on over here and take a look for yourself," I said.

She flopped around on the bed like a great female walrus and come on over to stand beside me, and then she looked down, and she seen him too. He was just getting off his horse right down below us at the hitch rail in front of Harvey's Hooch House, what me and Bonnie owned together. We was business partners, you see.

"Who's that?" she said.

"Hell if I know," I said. "I never set eyes on the son of a bitch before, but he's a mean one, I can tell you that just by looking."

"How do you know that if you don't even know who he is?" she asked me.

"By his guns and his clothes," I said. "By the way he rides and the way he moves. Hell, if that ole boy ain't a professional gunfighter, I'll kiss your puckering ass three times a day for the next month. Hell, it's my business to know them kind. Pour them drinks, will you, sweets?"

I went to pulling my clothes on then, and ole Bonnie went on over to pour the drinks. She was still nekkid when she handed me mine, but I had my britches on. I tuck a slug of that good stuff and set the glass down. Then I finished dressing. Bonnie had commenced to flouncing around, pulling her own clothes on. She was about as anxious as me to find out who the sinister stranger downstairs was. I was a-wondering what kind of trouble he might be, and I could only imagine what the hell she was a-wondering about him. I had me a few ideas on that subject, though.

Final I got my gunbelt strapped on and put the hat on my head, and I tuck my glass up again and drained it down all in a gulp. I set the glass down and started for the door.

"Hold on, Barjack," Bonnie said. "Wait up for me."

"Well, goddamn it," I said, "get a wiggle on." Then I thought that was a silly thing for me to say to her, 'cause ever' time she moved she wiggled all over. If ole Bonnie had ever been slim, it had been way before I ever knowed her. She was ample, and I liked her thataway. It was just all that much more to get ahold of and to fool around with. And she did enjoy the fooling, I can tell you that. I pulled a cigar outa my pocket and stuck it in my mouth, mainly so I'd have me something to do while I waited for her to cover up all of her bulk, and then I pulled out a match and struck it and fired up my smoke. Final, she was dressed.

"Okay," she said, flouncing over towards me. I turned around and pulled open the door, and we headed on out into the hallway, down to the top of the stairs, and started down into the main room of the Hooch House. I seen him right away. He was setting all by his lonesome at a table in the back of the room, and he was a-drinking coffee. I could tell he was watching the room real careful-like, too. Me and Bonnie went to the bar, and ole Aubrey come over to us.

"You want your regular?" he said.

"Yeah," I said. "Her, too."

I was looking in the mirror at the gunfighter across the room. Aubrey brung us our drinks, mine in a big tumbler, and I picked it up and turned around, putting my elbows up on the bar. I made sure that my coat was open so that the star on my vest was a-showing. I couldn't tell though that the stranger was paying no mind about it.

"Let's go say howdy," I said to Bonnie.

She smiled real wide and twitched around a bit and said, "Okay."

Me and her walked back toward the gunslinger's table. He seen us, all right. He didn't make no moves nor nothing, but I knowed that he was ready for anything what might happen. He was eyeballing us over the edge of his cup as he sipped his coffee. We come on up to the table and stopped.

"Howdy," I said.

He nodded.

"My name's Barjack," I went on. "I'm the town marshal of this here town, and I'm also part owner of this establishment you're a-setting in. This here lady with me is Miss Bonnie Boodle. She's my business partner here."

"Howdy, ma'am," he said, giving a slight nod to Bonnie.

"We're pleased to have you here," she said.

The stranger looked over at me.

"Is that a unanimous sentiment?" he asked me.

His big words kinda throwed me for a second, so I just said, "If you mean am I glad to have you here too, well, now, that all depends on a few things."

"What does it depend on?" he said.

"Well, if you're a-talking to me as a businessman," I said, "I'd have to say that a new customer is always welcome here. If you're a-talking to me as the town marshal of Asininity, then I'd have to know your name and what your business is in our little peaceable town."

"My name's Herman Sly," he said, "and I'm just looking for a place to rest up for a while. That's all. I'm glad to hear that it's a peaceable town. Does that satisfy the marshal in you?"

I harrumphed a bit and hitched my britches. "Well," I said, "I reckon it does. For now."

"Now may I speak to the businessman?" Sly said.

"Well, yeah," I said. "Sure. Go ahead. Shoot."

It come to me that I had picked a unfortunate word for my last one just then, and it also come to me that I was likely acting more than a bit nervous. I tried to get ahold of myself.

"Do you have rooms to rent in this establishment?" he asked.

"Well, yeah," I said. "We got rooms. They ain't exactly fancy hotel rooms, though, if you get my meaning."

"That's all right," he said. "I have simple tastes. Where can I get a good meal?"

"Over across the street at the White Owl Supper Club," I said. "It's my wife's . . . establishment. Well, uh, Bonnie, why don't you take care a the gentleman's needs? I got me some work to do over in the marshaling office."

I give the "gentleman" a quick tip of the brim of my hat and turned around and hurried outa there. I walked fast down to the office, thinking all the time that I had ought to know who the hell that bastard was. Like I done said, I had never saw him before, but then the name he give was a-buzzing in the back of my head. Herman Sly. Herman Sly. I went into the office, and my depitty, ole Happy Bonapart, jerked his legs offa my desk real quick-like and jumped up outa my chair. He moved out from behind my big desk and over against the wall.

"Howdy, Barjack," he said.

"How many times I got to tell you to set in your own

12

chair?" I grumbled at him. He never answered, but then, I never really expected him to. I went on behind the desk and set my ass down. I jerked open a drawer and tuck out a bottle and a glass and poured myself a drink. I tuck a healthy swig and set the glass down. Then I jerked open another drawer and pulled out a big stack of dodgers and commenced to looking through them. I never seen no picture of Herman Sly, though, and I never come across his name neither.

"What you looking for, Barjack?" Happy asked me.

"Herman Sly," I said.

"Herman Sly?" Happy said.

"Goddamn it," I said, "you heard me. How come you always repeat something like that? I'm a-looking for Herman Sly, or anything on Herman Sly I can find out, but he ain't in here nowheres."

"That's 'cause nothing's never been proved against him," Happy said. "He ain't never been charged with no crime."

"You know about him?" I said.

"Well, yeah," Happy said. "I heard some things."

"Well, tell me, you silly little runt," I said. "Do I got to drag it outa you or what?"

"He's a killer," said Happy. "A real professional gunfighter. He don't kill no one but only when he's been paid to do it. And then, they say, he always goads the other feller into pulling first, so he can claim self-defense. No telling how many men he's kilt, but he ain't never been charged with nothing. It's always self-defense. The other feller's always drawed first. Hell, Barjack, he's famous. Why, they call him the Widow-maker, and the Undertaker, and a whole bunch a other such-like names. Ain't you never heard of him?"

"A course I have," I said. "That's how I come to be looking for information on him."

"Well, you ain't going to find none," Happy said, "on account of all what I just told you. He ain't wanted nor nothing like that."

"I just couldn't quite call it all to mind," I said. "That's all."

"How come you to be a-looking for him like that?" Happy asked me.

I picked up my glass and tuck me another drink. "He's here, Happy," I said. "He's right over there at the Hooch House right now, setting there bigger'n hell."

"The Widowmaker's at the Hooch House?" Happy said.

"There you go again," I said. "I wouldn'ta said it if it weren't true. He's over there all right, and he's a-getting hisself a room. He means to stay for a spell."

"How long?" Happy asked me.

"He wouldn't say," I told him. "Just for a spell."

"Well, what's he doing here?" said Happy.

"He's a-looking for a quiet place to rest up, he says," I said.

"Do you believe him?"

"I ain't sure."

"I wonder who he's come after," Happy said, but he said it like he was a-talking to hisself, like as if he was just a-thinking out loud.

"He never said he come after no one," I said. "Even a killer's got to rest, don't he?"

"Not the Undertaker," Happy said. "He's come here

to do a job. I bet you. He's got someone to kill. Reckon who it might be?"

"Hell," I said, "even if you're right, it could be anyone. Ain't no way we could figger that one out. Ever'one's got enemies somewhere. And he sure ain't going to tell us, even if we was to ask him."

"It'd have to be someone with enough money to pay what he gets," Happy said, "and from what all I've heard, he don't work cheap."

"Happy, you little son of a bitch," I said, "I don't want to hear no more of that kinda talk. You hear me? Goddamn it, I mean it. If I hear any more of that kinda talk outa you, I'll stomp the crap outa your dumb ass. You hear me?"

"I hear you, Barjack," he said, but by the look on his silly face, I knowed he was still a-trying to figger out just who it was what ole Sly had come to town to kill.

I picked up my drink and tuck myself another slug of it. Goddamn, it was good stuff. 'Course, I only bought the best, and always my favorite brand, too. Most usually I done my drinking down at the Hooch House, but just in case I was to have to go to work at my marshaling office, I always kept me a bottle stashed in there, too. I was taking me another good drink when I seen ole Happy a-moving toward the door. I brung the glass down quick-like and swallered hard.

"Where the hell you going?" I asked him.

"Thought I'd just stroll over to the Hooch House," Happy said.

"And get yourself a look at that widow-making son of a bitch?" I said.

"Well," he said, "I would kinda like to get a look and

15

see for myself just what he looks like," said Happy.

"All right, you go right on ahead," I said, "but you just keep in mind—well, hell, I ain't sure you got no mind—you just remember what I said. No more talk about who is it that the Undertaker come to town to kill. He's just here to take hisself a rest. That's all. Keep your goddamn mouth shut, or I'll squash your head in—and I mean it, too."

"Hell, Barjack," he said, "I know you that well. I know you mean it. I won't say nothing. I just want to get me a look. That's all."

Ole Happy, he went on out, and I set down heavy in my chair. I sure as hell didn't want to create no panic in Asininity, what with the Widowmaker hisself in town. Herman Sly. Herman Sly hisself in person. In the flesh. I tuck another drink, and I set my glass down. Who the hell, I said to myself, just who the hell has he come to town to kill? Why, hell. It could be me. I had damn sure made me a passel of enemies over the years. There was them Five-Pointers from New York City from way back when I was just a snot-nosed kid. And there was kin and friends of the Bensons. Well, I modified that one a bit. I couldn't believe that they'd ever had no friends, but they could sure enough have more kin. Same way with them Marlins. And then there was my own former deppity, ole Texas Jack, what I had been forced to kill that time.

Then I commenced to thinking closer to home. Ole Bonnie hadn't never really forgive me for getting married up to Lillian, and if I was to get knocked off, why, she'd have the whole entire Hooch House all to herself. And Bonnie had tried to kill me more than once. I didn't really think that Bonnie woulda hired no damn Undertaker to do me in, though. I figgered Bonnie to do the job her own self if she was to ever take it in mind again. But Lillian, now there was a lady what wouldn't want to get her own hands bloody, and I reckoned that she had reasons aplenty to want to have me put away for final.

Just to begin with, why, she'd wind up owning ever'thing what I owned. And then, she likely weren't too happy with my dallying around with ole Bonnie right there under her nose, so to speak, even though she never let on she knowed nothing about it. Yeah, I begun to think that just maybe ole Lillian had somehow or other got ahold of the Widowmaker and paid him to make a widow outa her, and that was the reason that ole Herman Sly had come a-riding into town. The thought made me just a mite nervous till I brung back to mind what ole Happy had said. The Undertaker never draws first. He goads his victims into drawing on him, and then he kills them and calls it self-defense. Well, hell, I told myself, I just won't draw on the son of a bitch. I'll stand right there and let him call me five hundred kinds of coward and chicken, and the only thing I'll do is just only take me another drink of whiskey. I can handle that all right. Ain't no slick gunfighter going to buffalo me. No sir.

I tuck another drink and then left the office. I was headed back for the Hooch House, but outside I seen Happy headed for the White Owl. I changed my course so as to intercept him. "Where the hell you going now?" I asked him.

"They told me at the Hooch House that ole Sly had

come over here for a steak dinner," Happy said. "I ain't got me a look at him yet."

I turned to walk along with Happy. "You just remember to keep your damn mouth shut," I said. Whenever we walked into the White Owl, right away I seen ole Lillian a-hovering over a table and ole Sly a-setting there a-drinking coffee. I led Happy right on over to that table.

"Well, Mr. Sly," I said, "I see you've done met my wife there."

"I've had the honor," Sly said. Oh, he was a slick one, a real smooth talker.

"This here is Happy Bonapart," I said. "He's my de-pitty."

"How do you do, Mr. Bonapart," Sly said, and I remember thinking that I hadn't never in all the years I had knowed ole Happy knowed anyone else to ever say that there mister word in front of Happy's name. Well, ole Happy, he whipped the hat offa the top of his head and grinned.

"How do you do, sir," he said. It like to made me want to puke.

"Lillian," I said, "me and ole Happy need us a drink."

"You know where to find it, Barjack," she said, and her voice had that icy chill on it what she seemed to reserve just only for me. She was really a-putting on the dog for ole Sly, though, and she sure as hell didn't like me interrupting it, I could tell that, and she didn't like me bringing my sloppy ass into her fancy place neither, 'specially not when she had herself a customer what she was a trying to impress. The thought crept into my head again that maybe it was ole Lillian what had sent for Mister Sly in the first place so that he could make her into a genuine widow woman. My skin kinda crawled a bit on that one, with him just a-setting right there in the same room with me and her both.

"Come on, Happy," I said, and I led the way over to the bar. I went on around behind it and got us each a glass, and I hauled out my bottle and poured us a drink. Then I leaned across the bar and spoke real low to Happy.

"Well," I said, "you seen him now. What do you think?"

Happy whispered back to me, "He's here to kill someone, Barjack. Mark my words."

Chapter Two

I didn't stick around the White Owl too long after that. It weren't my kinda place nohow. It suited my Lillian's fancy, and I just kept it open and kept supporting it with money from the Hooch House just only to keep her sorta happy and offa my back. That's all. I didn't let ole Happy stick around, neither. I made him walk back on over to the Hooch House with me, and me and him set down with ole Bonnie and commenced to drinking some more whiskey.

"Well," ole Bonnie said, "what d'ya think, Barjack?"

" 'Bout what?" I said, and of course I knowed right well just what it was she was a-talking about, but I weren't in no good mood.

"About that killer," she said. "What else?"

"He ain't wanted," I said, "and he's just in town for a rest-up. That's all. That's what he told me, and I ain't

20

got no reason to disbelieve him. Ain't nothing for me to think about. Nor you, neither." I turned on ole Happy then. "Nor you. And I don't want to hear no scary talk from neither one of you. I mean that. I don't want no panic in this town 'cause of him being here."

I tuck me a big gulp of whiskey outa my tumbler, and Bonnie leaned over close to me and said, "But what if he lied to you, Barjack? What if he did come here to kill someone?"

"Who?" I said. "Who the hell is there in this puny town important enough for someone to pay the price it takes to hire on the goddamn Widowmaker?"

"Well, I don't know," she said.

"It ain't got to be someone important," Happy said. "It just gots to be someone that someone else is pissed off at enough to pay the price. That's all."

"And there's assholes aplenty around here," Bonnie added. "Why, hell, it could be most anyone. I reckon I've even made my enemies along the line."

"The Widowmaker ain't never shot a woman," Happy said.

"Well," said Bonnie, "that's a comfort. 'Course, like they say, there's a first time for ever'thing."

I didn't say nothing, but I was thinking about ole Texas Jack and the Bensons and the Marlins and few others—even the ole Five-Pointers, and I was a-wondering about any surviving kin or friends any of them might have. It come to me that the Marlins could have it in for ole Happy too, but it weren't likely they'd have it in as bad for him as they did for me. Just then ole Sam Hooper come walking in the place. As he

walked by the table where we was a-setting, he tipped
his hat.

"Howdy, Miss Bonnie," he said. "Barjack. Happy."

We all howdied him back, and he bellied up to the
bar, where ole Aubrey tuck care of him by bringing out
his favorite whiskey. Ole Sam was particular 'bout his
whiskey, as any good drinking man ought to be. He
could afford to be thataway, too. He owned one of the
biggest cattle operations in the whole damn territory. He
never come into town too often, but whenever he did
come in, why, hell, ever'one kowtowed to his ass just
in case he might sprinkle some of his money in their
direction. Ever'one but me. I always figgered that I was
just as good a man as the next, money or no, and by
this time of my life, I weren't doing too bad in that
money area neither.

"I hope there ain't no trouble in here tonight," Bonnie
said real low.

"Trouble?" I said. "What kinda trouble? What're you
talking about?"

She didn't say nothing then. She just kinda nodded
her head toward the back corner of the room, off to my
right side, and I turned around and give a look. I hadn't
noticed before, but there was ole Silver Spike Hanlon a-
setting back there with a couple of his cowhands.

Hanlon and Hooper had been at each other's throats
for years. Hell, it had been so long that no one even
could recollect what it was had set them off like that in
the first place. They just hated each other's guts all the
way to hell and back. That's all they was to it. Hanlon's
spread weren't quite as big as Hooper's, but it was big
enough. The two most richest and powerfullest ranchers

around was always just on the verge of starting a god-danm range war with each other.

"Don't worry," I said. "If them two bastards start anything in here, I'll finish it for them."

"That's what I'm worried about," Bonnie said.

I chose to ignore that insulting remark on account of ole Bonnie just natural liked to insult me, and besides that, I had more important things on my mind. Anyhow, there weren't no trouble, 'cause in just another minute or so, ole Hanlon tossed down his whiskey and stood up.

"Come on, boys," he said to his cowhands. "Let's get the hell outa this place. I ain't quite content with the company in here."

They walked out without saying nothing else, and ole Hooper, he never even turned his head to look at them as they walked right past him. 'Course, he didn't really have to turn his head to see them. They was a big mirror behind the bar, and he was a-facing that. He could see them in there, all right. But they left, and he never paid no mind. Bonnie heaved a big sigh like she was real relieved, but me, I was actual kinda disappointed. The mood I was in, I coulda used some interesting diversion.

In just a little bit after that, I noticed that it was about time for ole Lillian to shut down the White Owl, and so I drunk down the rest of the whiskey outa my glass and got up and left the Hooch House. I walked on back over to the White Owl and found Lillian just a-putting out all the lights. "What are you doing here, Barjack?" she said.

"I just thought I'd come on over and walk you home," I said. "That's all."

She give me a real suspicious look at that and said, "Why?"

"Well," I said, "it's a-getting dark earlier this time of year, and we got us some dangerous folks in town right now. I just thought it might give you some comfort."

"Well, all right," she said. She put out the last light, and I follered her out the door. She locked it up, and we headed for the house. I weren't looking forward too much to seeing the damn kid, but I strolled along with her anyhow.

"You know who that son of a bitch was?" I asked her. "The one you was making so much over?"

"Who are you talking about?" she said, as if she didn't have no idea what the hell I was a-talking about.

"That slick stranger you was hovering over while he was eating his steak," I said. "Black suit and all. Smooth talker. Using them fancy words."

"You mean Mister Sly?" she said.

"So you do know who he is," I said, kinda accusing-like.

"He introduced himself," she said. "He's a gentleman. I don't see many of them around this town."

I tuck that jab in stride too. It come to me, though, that ole Lillian and ole Bonnie had a hell of a lot more in common than what most folks would ever notice by just only a-looking at them.

"He's a famous professional killer," I said. "They call him the Widowmaker and the Undertaker and all other kinds of killer names. He's killed forty or fifty, maybe a hunderd men. He's cold blooded, and he does it just for money. That's all. Killing's a business with him."

"Well," Lillian said in her iciest cold voice, "why don't you arrest him, then?"

" 'Cause he ain't wanted," I said. "That's why. He always makes the other feller draw first, and then he kills him dead with just only one shot. He ain't wanted."

"Then he's not a criminal," she said, "and I'm pleased to have him as a customer. He'll be back in the morning for breakfast. I'm looking forward to it."

"Damn it, woman," I said. "Ain't you been listening to what I'm telling you? He's a cold-blooded, murdering son of a bitch."

"Murder's against the law, Barjack," she said. "You just told me that Mister Sly is not a wanted man. You need to get your story straight."

We was just coming up to the house, and ole Lillian was frustrating the hell outa me, and I thought about the snot-nosed kid inside, and I just throwed up my hands and turned away. "Hell," I said, "I'm going back to the Hooch House."

Lillian didn't say nothing. She just walked on in the house and slammed the door. I shivered a bit, and I weren't sure if it was from the chill in the night air or from the worser one coming offa my wife. I started in to walking back to the Hooch House. When I final got there and went back inside, I seen that ole Happy was bellied up to the bar beside ole Hooper, and goddamned if ole Bonnie weren't setting at a table with the Widow-maker hisself. That burned my ass. Here both my women was a-making up to the son of a bitch. I moved up beside Happy.

"Aubrey," I said, "give me a whiskey, goddamn it."

"You just got here, Barjack," Aubrey said. "You don't need to go cussing me."

He put my tumbler and my bottle both up on the bar in front a me, and he poured the tumbler might' near full. He knowed how I liked it, all right.

"I ain't cussing you, Aubrey," I said. "I'm just a-cussing in general. The world is full of crap. Leastways, it is in these parts."

"You ain't just now figgering that one out, are you?" he said.

"I guess I'm just a-noticing it a little more today," I said. "That's all."

Aubrey leaned across the bar and spoke to me in a real low voice, giving me a kinda knowing look at the same time. "The Widowmaker?" he said.

I give Happy a hard, accusing look.

"I never said nothing," he said.

I put my elbow on the bar and my head in my hand. "Goddamn it," I said. "Does the whole town know by now?"

"What was that?" Hooper said. I had damn near forgot that he was a-standing there just on the other side of Happy. I looked up real quick and seen Hooper giving me a straight on serious look.

"Nothing," I said. "Never mind."

Hooper, he looked up in the mirror where he had a clear view of ole Bonnie and Sly a-setting there at a table. He stared at them for a few seconds. Then, "Of course," he said. "That's Herman Sly. The Widowmaker. What's he doing here, Barjack?"

"How should I know?" I said.

"You ought to know," Hooper said. "It's your business to know. You're the town marshal, and he's trouble. You ought to know."

"I done had a talk with him," I said. "He ain't here on business. He's here to take him a rest. That's all. Hell, even killers got to rest, ain't they? Forget it."

"That's what he would say, of course," said Hooper. "He never admits that he went to a place deliberately to kill someone. You run him out of town, Barjack. Right now."

"Now, don't go telling me how to do my marshaling job, Sam," I said. "He ain't wanted, and he ain't broke no laws around here. I got no cause to run him outa town. If you can't stand being in the same town with him, just go on back home to your big-ass ranch."

"I'm going," he said, "and the next time you see me, I'll have some boys with me, and we'll all be armed, too."

He stormed right on outa there.

"He's mad," said Happy.

"No kidding," I said.

"You reckon he's afeared that Sly has come after him?" Happy asked me.

"Could be," I said. "I reckon he's made his share of enemies over the years."

I was thinking that I hoped ole Sly had come after Hooper. Hell, it wouldn't bother me none to see Sly gun Hooper down, the way ole Hooper was a-talking at me. I don't reckon I would a give a damn. I wouldn't do nothing about it, neither, 'cause as long as Sly kept true to his old pattern, why, he'd make Hooper draw first, and then all I'd have to do is just write it down as self-defense and forget about it. Then the whole thing would be over with, and Sly would move on, and things would be back to normal around my little town. Anyhow, Hooper walked out and Sly never paid no mind to him. I turned around and looked at Sly. Bonnie was leaning over into him real cozy-like. I knowed what she was up to. I poured my tumbler back full, picked it up, and headed toward their table.

"Barjack," said Happy. "Be careful."

I ignored him and walked on back there, and I stood there a-looking down at the two of them. "How do, Mister Sly," I said.

"Good evening, Marshal," he said.

Oh, how his slickery words pissed me off.

"Well, now," I said, "might I have the pleasure of joining you two here at your table for your fine company? If you don't mind too much."

"Sit down, Marshal," Sly said. "Please."

I set, and I tuck me a gulp of my whiskey. I give ole Bonnie a hard look, and she just ignored it and looked up at ole Sly real goggly-eyed.

"I had a very good steak at Mrs. Barjack's establishment," Sly said. "Thank you for directing me there."

"Ain't nothing special," I said. "It all goes into my pocket eventual. 'Course, ole Lillian, she spends it all."

Sly give a kinda polite chuckle that irritated the hell outa me. I tuck me another drink. Ole Bonnie give me the eye. "Barjack," she said, "what the hell're you up to?"

"I ain't up to nothing, Bonnie," I said. "I just thought that I'd take this here opportunity to get a little more acquainted with our visitor here. That's all. I done found out that he had hisself a nice supper, and I'm right glad to hear it. Whenever I walked my wife home just now, she told me that he was a perfect gentleman, and I'm glad to know that too. Don't go suspicioning me of no sinister motives, now."

"I'm glad to have the marshal's company, Miss Boodle," Sly said, and I kinda cringed.

"Is there anything you need what we ain't provided?" I asked him.

"I could use a bath before retiring," he said, "if it isn't too much trouble."

"I reckon ole Bonnie here could see to that," I said, "couldn't you, ole gal?"

She looked a little bit disappointed, and she give him a cow-eyed look and said, "Do you want it right away?"

"I am a little tired," he said. "I would like to call it a day soon."

"I'll fix it up," she said, and she give me another of them hard looks as she was a-getting up to go tend to her business. I waited a bit till she was outa earshot, and then I said, "Sly, I know who you are."

"I made no secret of it," he said.

"You didn't say you was the Undertaker or the Widowmaker," I accused him.

"Those are names I've been called," he said. "I've been called worse. I don't introduce myself by names I've been called. My name is Herman Sly."

"Whatever," I said.

"What did you expect, Marshal?" he said. "Should I have come in here and announced that I'm a notorious gunfighter? All I want is a few days of peace and quiet. That's all. Is there anything wrong with that?"

"No," I said, "if you're a-telling me the truth."

"Why should I lie?" he said.

" 'Cause you ain't never been caught doing no murder," I said. " 'Cause if you was to come into a town and announce your intentions of killing someone, you might be charged with a-murdering. But if you come in saying that you just want a few days of peace and quiet, and then you locate the poor son of a bitch you been paid to kill and goad him into a gunfight and he draws first and you kill him, you can go on pretending you didn't come to town for no such a purpose. That's how come you might lie about it. Now, I never said you lied. I only just said that's how come you might lie."

"I take your point, Marshal," he said. "But please rest assured that I have not lied to you. I stopped off in your town for a much-needed rest. That's all."

"You ain't had nothing to drink but coffee since you been here," I said. "You trying to keep alert, are you?"

"I always try to stay alert," Sly said. "I'm still alive."

"Have a drink with me," I said.

He looked at me, and I tell you, his eyes was steely. A cold chill run through me clean into my bones, and I asked myself how come I had done such a stupid thing. Hell, I had damn near accused him of lying to me, and I had come close to challenging the son of a bitch.

"All right," he said.

I waved an arm at ole Aubrey and had him bring another glass, and then I poured ole Sly a drink from out of my own special bottle. I shoved it across the table at him. He picked it up, and I picked up mine, and I held it up like as if for a toast, you know. Sly lifted his glass and clinked it against mine.

"To a good rest," I said.

"To a happy and peaceful visit," he added.

We each tuck a gulp, and I watched him over my glass as I drunk. I don't know quite what it was I was a-watching for, but whatever it was, it never happened. He drunk that whiskey like it was water. Whenever we both finished our tumblers full, I poured us another. After two full tumblers, I loosened up some. He seemed just the same as before. 'Course, I had been a-drinking most all day long.

"Sly," I said, "is it true what they say about you?"

"I don't know," he said. "What do they say?"

"They say you've killed nigh onto a hunderd men," I said.

"That's a gross exaggeration," he said.

"They say you kill for money," I said. "Someone wants someone else killed, and he pays you a fat fee, and you just go out and kill that poor son of a bitch for him. Course, they say, you push the other feller into going for his gun first, and then you kill him and claim self-defense. You collect your money just the same. That's what they say."

"A man makes his living the best way he can," Sly said.

He was sly, all right. He only sort of answered my question.

"But you ain't here to kill no one?" I said.

"I was passing through your town," he said. "It seemed like a nice, quiet, peaceful little town, and I need a rest. That's the only reason I stopped here. Barjack, everywhere I go, my reputation precedes me. I can't help that. But a man needs a rest now and then. Even the Widowmaker needs a rest. Okay?"

I looked over and seen that his glass was empty, so I tipped mine up and emptied it. Then I poured us another. "Okay," I said. Well, we drunk that one, and we talked some more, and by and by ole Bonnie come a-flouncing down the stairs and back over to the table.

"Your bath is ready, Mister Sly," she said.

He stood up, and so did I.

"Well, whoop-ti-do," I said, and then I fell over backwards into my chair, and when I hit it, it fell over backward. I was laying on the floor with my legs still up over the damn chair, but even from that awkward position and with the room a-spinning some, I seen ole Sly walk straight and tall beside ole Bonnie a-heading for the stairs. By God, the bastard could hold his booze, and I liked him some better for that.

Chapter Three

Well, hell, I never got my own ass up from offa the floor
that night, not that I recall, and not on my own, I reckon.
I woke up sometime the next morning on a cot in one
of my own jail cells. I wouldn't even of woke up then,
I guess it was about midmorning, but I heard a cater-
wauling and a door slam, and I raised up my head with
a groan, 'cause it was a-throbbing some, I can tell you.
Well, it was ole Peester, our goddamned mayor, what
had come in on me in that rude manner. I set up a-
holding my head.

"What the hell is this I hear about a professional killer
in our midst?" he was a-saying.

"Calm down, Mayor," I said. "You're way too loud
for me this morning."

"I understand you have a man named Sly staying at
your establishment," he said. "They tell me he's a pro-

33

fessional killer, a gun for hire. Why haven't you run him out of town?"

"Now, Mayor," I said, calling up all the patience I had in me, "he ain't broke no laws and he ain't wanted. I got no call to be running him outa town."

"You mean you can't run him out just on his reputation?" Peester said.

"You're the damned pettifogging lawyer," I said. "You tell me. What if I was to tell him to get his ass outa town, and then he come to you with money for you to represent him. What the hell would you say to that?"

"Well, I—"

"You ain't got nothing to say now, do you?" I said. "You know goddamn well that I'm right."

"You could have told him that you were out of rooms." Peester said. "You could have done that at least."

"Well, I didn't, did I?" I said. My head was hurting me so bad that I was quick losing patience with ole Peester. I never much liked him nohow, but he paid my wages as town marshal so I just kinda put up with him. "Now, damn it, unless you shut the hell up about it, I'm a-fixing to toss your ass out onto the street. Who told you about ole Sly, anyhow?"

"Never mind about that," Peester said.

"Well, then, get the hell outa here," I said.

Peester grumbled his way back to the front door, and just as he jerked it open, he looked back over his shoulder and said, "You'd better handle this, Barjack. I'm warning you."

I jumped up and made like I was a-going after him, and he went out quick and slammed the door behind him. I stopped and set back down a-moaning. That fast motion had like to done me in. I set there a-holding my head for a minute or two, and then I got up slow-like and made my way over to my desk. I set down in my big chair and pulled open the desk drawer what held my tumbler and bottle, and I poured myself a healthy drink. A couple of swallers of that good stuff and I felt somewhat better.

I walked on over to the White Owl and had Lillian fix me up a breakfast. Well, she didn't do it herself. She had ole Horace a-cooking back in the kitchen, but she brung it out to me and tossed the plate down in front of me with a thunk. "That the way you served up ole Sly's breakfast this morning?" I said.

"He's a gentleman," she said.

"Well, I'm your goddamned husband," I said.

"You might try acting like it now and then," she said. Damn but she was icy. I just tuck into my breakfast and tried to ignore her attitude. I et it all and slurped up one cup of coffee, and I had done had my fill of the White Owl. I left outa there and went on over to the Hooch House, where I was more at home. First off I seen ole Happy, and I give him a scowl.

"How come you ain't minding the office?" I said.

He jumped right up. "I'm a-going over there right now," he said.

Sly was setting at the same back table he'd been at the night before, and he was a-sipping coffee just like before. Just about then, I seen ole Bonnie a-flopping her way downstairs. It was just about her usual time for getting up and around. There weren't no one else in the place, 'cept for ole Aubrey back behind the bar. I had him bring me some coffee, since I had got me only one cup with my breakfast.

"Good morning, Marshal Barjack," Sly said.

I looked back at him and nodded my head.

"Join me?" he said.

I picked up my coffee cup and made my way back to the table where he was a-setting, and I pulled out a chair and plopped my old ass down in it. "You don't look no worse for the wear," I said. "I hadn't figgered you for a drinking man."

"Oh," he said, "I didn't put away nearly as much as you did last night."

"I had a early start," I said, and I lifted my cup and tuck a long noisy sip of coffee. 'Bout then ole Bonnie come a-bouncing over to us. Sly stood up and tuck his hat off. I wrenched up my face at that and just tuck me another sip a coffee.

"Good morning, Miss Boodle," he said. "Would you care to join us?"

"I'd be charmed," Bonnie said, and I groaned. She plopped her ass down and smiled a simpering smile at him, and Aubrey come along a-fetching her coffee to her. "Thank you, Aubrey, dear," she said.

"You getting that rest you was a-looking for?" I asked Sly.

"Yes," he said. "So far. I had a good night's sleep last night, and this morning has been quiet enough."

"I'm glad to hear it," I said, " 'cause I sure ain't. I've done had all kinds of folks a-coming at me wanting to know what the hell you're a-doing in town and how come I ain't run you out. You just being here makes my job twice as bad as normal. It's like you said last night.

Your reputation goes out in front of you, and even if you really ain't fixing to cause no trouble, your reputation does it all for you."

"You want me to leave town, Marshal?" he asked me, and he looked right into my eyes with his cold, steely gray ones.

"It'd make my life a hell of a lot easier," I said.

"If I don't go on my own," he said, "do you mean to run me out?"

"You ain't done nothing to give me no cause," I said.

"And I don't intend to," he said. "Barjack, I don't even know anyone in your town."

"You don't got to know them, do you?" I said. "You get a name, and you just go out and find him. Ain't that right?"

"I've got no name for this town," he said.

"Well, I hope you ain't joshing me," I said, and I slurped down the rest of my coffee. Then I hollered at ole Aubrey and told him to bring me a drink. I reckoned I'd had enough coffee to be wide awake. I was ready for something to get me a-going now for real. He brung me over a full tumbler and set it down in front of me, and just then ole Rumproast Thompson come in through the front door. I heard the door and looked around, and I could see that he was a-looking for trouble. He spotted Sly right off, and he stopped and crouched like as if he was ready to pull iron.

"Sly," he said. "You son of a bitch. Go for your gun."

"I got no reason," Sly said. "I don't even know you."

"I know you come here a-looking for me," Rumproast said. "I'm Jory Thompson. They call me Rumproast. I know who sent you, too. Come on. Get it over with."

"I don't know what you're talking about, boy," said Sly.

"I ain't going to draw first," Rumproast said. "I know what they say about you. But you're going to have to draw first on me, 'cause I ain't going to fall for that trick. You watch him, Barjack. If he comes out alive, it ain't going to be self-defense. I ain't pulling first. Go on, you chicken son of a bitch."

"I'm going up to my room," Sly said. He pushed back his chair, and Rumproast jerked out his six-shooter. Aubrey fell flat on the floor. Rumproast just only had his shooter up halfway when I heard the roar of Sly's gun. He was a-holding it under the table, and his shot cut into Rumproast's thigh. Rumproast yowled out and fell down on the floor. Sly stood up and pulled his shooter out from under the table. He leveled it at ole Rumproast. Rumproast was still a-clutching his own, but it weren't lifted up. It was just pointed at the floor is all.

"Put it down," Sly said.

Rumproast raised it up a little. He was a-thinking about it.

"Don't do it, boy," Sly said. "It's not worth it."

Rumproast made up his mind right quick and raised that gun, and Sly squeezed off another one. This time his lead smashed Rumproast's right shoulder. I got up and walked over there and kicked his gun across the floor.

"You damn fool," I said. "Aubrey, get your ass up offa the floor and go fetch the doc. Then get Happy."

Aubrey got up a-trembling and headed for the door. Just then Happy come a-running in.

"Here's Happy," Aubrey said.

"I can see that," I said, "Go on."

Aubrey run on out. Rumproast was just a-laying on the floor a-moaning and bleeding. Sly had holstered his gun, and he walked over to stand beside me.

"Do you need me?" he said.

"Naw, hell," I said. "Go on."

He went upstairs without looking back.

"Rumproast, you dumb fool," I said. "You're damn lucky to be alive. And by the way, you being alive after you went and pulled on him first proves that he weren't lying to you. If it was you he was after, you'd be dead right now."

"I'm hurting here, Barjack," he said.

"Serves you right," I said. The doc come in then, and he seen Rumproast there staining my floor, and went on over to tend to him. I turned to Happy. "When Doc's done here," I said, "take ole Rumproast over to a cell to heal up."

"What's the charge, Barjack?" Happy said.

"Disturbing the peace," I said. "Commencing a gun-fight. Attempted killing. Hell, there's a whole passel of them. Take your pick or use them all. I don't give a damn."

I walked back to the table where I had left my tumbler of good whiskey, and I set my ass down again. Bonnie was still just a-setting there. "My God," she said. "That man is fast."

"I reckon," I said.

"Like greased lightning," she said.

"He's a fair hand with a gun," I said.

"Fair?" she said. "Who you seen better?"

"Hell, Bonnie, I seen them all," I said. "They's always

someone faster, and they all dies the same way, eventual." The truth was that I was just about as impressed as ole Bonnie was. I hadn't never seen no one better than ole Sly. Hell, he was fast and accurate enough that he didn't even have to kill ole Rumproast in order to keep his own self from getting killed, and that's pretty damn good. If it'd been me there in ole Sly's place, why, I'da had to of killed ole Rumproast. I weren't good enough to be choicey like that. I tuck me another slug of whiskey, and then I said, "Don't be going goggly-eyed over no damn gunfighter."

Bonnie kinda wiggled around, and her titties wobbled something fierce. She leaned toward me with a silly little grin on her face, and she said. "You jealous, Barjack?"

"Hell, no," I said. "I ain't jealous a that slicker." I tuck me another drink. "You give him his bath last night, did you?"

"Wouldn't you like to know?" she said, still a-grinning like that. I thought about slapping that damn grin offa her face, but I figgered that if I was to do that, why, she'd just slip up behind me later with a bottle and bash me in the head.

"I don't give a damn what you washed," I said.

"Well, I never," she said, and a pout set in on her face. She was real ugly whenever that tuck place. "He wouldn't even take off his shirt till I left the room, and then he locked the door."

I wondered if I was going to have to issue another challenge to get him to climb onto ole Bonnie the way I done to get him to take a drink, but then I thought if he tuck to it the way he tuck to drink, he'd be at it for three days. I decided to let well enough just be. Bonnie reached over and kinda tickled me under the chin. "Now, cut that out, ole gal," I said.

"I don't wash no one but just only you," she said. "You want a bath, Barjack? You need one."

"I don't need no bath this time of the day," I said. "What if something was to call me to my marshaling duties and me a-laying up there nekkid in a tub of suds?"

She commenced to rubbing her great fleshiness all over me just then, and to reaching all over with her hands, too, at the same time, and I kinda felt a hot flush on my face. I picked up my tumbler and drunk it dry. "Come on, sweets," I said. "I need me a bath."

We was upstairs for a spell, and whenever we come back down, I was clean as a pin, and I was feeling some spry from the romping I'd had me with ole Bonnie. I come a-tripping on down the stairs like I was forty pounds lighter than what I really was, and Bonnie, she was a-hanging on my arm all the way, tits just a-bouncing. God, when them things done thataway, I wondered how they managed to stay attached to her chest.

Anyhow, as we was stepping down onto the floor I seen ole George Thompson a-coming through the door. That was Rumproast's daddy. Goddamn, I thought. Here's more trouble a-coming my way, and that just when I was in such a good mood, too. I shuck Bonnie loose from my arm and walked toward the bar. Ole George met me there, and he had a real stern look on his old face.

"I heard my boy got hisself shot in here today," he said.

"That's right, George," I said, "but he ain't dead, so don't go starting no trouble."

"Sounds to me like the trouble's done been started," he said. "I aim to finish it."

"George," I said, "your boy ain't too bright. You know that. He come in here accusing a man of wanting to kill him, and he kept calling for the man to draw down on him. The man wouldn't do it. Final, the man gets up to go to his room, and ole Rumproast, he just pulls his gun. Well, the man was faster. That's all. And what's more, deliberate, the man didn't kill him, so you ought to be grateful to the man for saving ole Rumproast's life for you. That's what you oughta be."

"You sure that's how it was?" George said.

"I was setting right there a-watching the whole damn thing," I said.

"Hell," George said, "if that boy weren't shot up, I'd give him a good whupping. Where's he at?"

"He's over in my jail," I said.

"I'll just go get him and take him on home," said George.

"I don't think you'd oughta do that just yet," I said. "You see, I had him charged with trying to do a killing and several other things, too. Besides, he's shot up pretty bad, and he's a hell of a lot closer to the doc over there in my jail than what he would be way out there at your place. You just go on over there and see him now if you want to, but just leave him in there for now. I figger his jail time oughta be just about as long as it takes for him to heal up real good."

George thought about that for a couple of seconds. Then he said, "Yeah. I see what you mean. Well, I'll just go on over there and see him."

"You just tell ole Happy that I said it's all right," I said.

"Yeah," said George, and he turned around and walked outa the Hooch House kinda slow with his shoulders slumped and his head a-hanging. Bonnie come up slow beside me.

"You took care of that real good, Barjack," she said.

"It's just all a part of my marshaling job," I said.

"Poor ole George," she said.

"Poor?" I said. "How come?"

"Well," she said, "his boy all shot up like that."

"His boy's alive," I said. "He's lucky ole George, I'd say. Unless you want to call him poor ole George on account of he's got such a dummy for a kid. Now, that's a reason for feeling sorry for him if you want one."

"Oh, Barjack," she said.

I walked on up to the bar, and I never even had to say nothing. Aubrey brung me a clean tumbler and a bottle, and he poured me a full glass. I tuck me a good swaller. It was just fine. Aubrey served up a drink for ole Bonnie too. She tuck a sip and then she hugged my arm again. "You want to go set, Barjack?" she said.

"Let's go," I said, and we went over to a table and set down. Just as we got settled, I seen ole Sly a-coming back down the stairs. He give me a look, and I nodded. Whenever he come close enough, I invited him to set with us and he did. He signaled Aubrey for coffee.

"You ain't in no mood for whiskey just yet?" I asked him.

"No," he said. "I'm not."

"You go up and get yourself some rest?" Bonnie said.

"Yes," he said. "In a sense."

"Hell," I said, "you don't need to rest up just from what you done a while ago. Do you?"

"I needed to relax my mind," Sly said. "I don't like what happened out here with that boy. It bothers me. It happens too often. No one will believe me when I say that I'm not after them."

"Why is that?" Bonnie said.

"They've all got enemies," said Sly. "They've all done something to someone, and when they see me, they think that their victims have sent me to even the score. It's the guilty conscience in all men. I bring it out. It's my curse."

"You're wrong about that," I said. "There ain't no guilty conscience in all men. I oughta know, 'cause I ain't got one."

"There's nothing you've done in your entire life that you feel guilty over?" Sly asked me.

"Not a damn thing," I said. "There's some stupid things I done that I feel stupid about, but that ain't guilty. No, sir."

"You're a fortunate man, Barjack," he said. "I'll modify my statement. Most men have guilty consciences. Some of us are even haunted by them."

Chapter Four

It weren't long after that when ole Peester come into the Hooch House. His face was red, and his chest was a-heaving. "Barjack," he said, real huffy-like, "I want to talk to you."

"If you want to talk to me about that there widow-making Herman Sly," I said, "he's a-setting right here at this table right with me right now, and you're a-looking at him. Is that what you was wanting to talk about, Peester?"

He started in to blustering and puffing and spitting all over his own fat belly. I ain't never seen a man back up so fast as what that shyster lawyer done just right at that time. So while he was a-trying to regain some control of his spit glands and his wagging tongue, I looked over at ole Sly.

"Mister Sly," I said, "this here is His Honor our mayor

of this here town. His name is Peester, and besides being the mayor he's a pettifogging lawyer." I leaned over real close to him then and lowered my voice some. "He's also a worthless son of a bitch," I added.

Ole Sly, he stood right up and offered out his hand to our mayor. "Mayor Peester," he said, "it's an honor, sir. My name is Herman Sly. I'm here in your peaceful town for a short visit. If you're concerned about the little episode that occurred in here recently, I regret it very much, and I assure you that I did everything I could to prevent it."

Peester allowed his hand to be shuck, but he never did find no more voice, not just then, and it come to me that I had witnessed a pure-dee miracle right there in the ole Hooch House, and what it was, it was a lawyer without no words. I wanted to hooraw out loud, but I never. Instead, I just set there and watched ole Peester turn around and walk outa the place still a-blustering and wheezing and kinda shaking his head.

Well, the day had gone by before I hardly knowed it. Sly got up to go over to the White Owl for his steak supper, and he asked me if I wanted to join him, but I declined. I poured me another glass of good whiskey and watched him walk out the door. I was thinking how it's funny the way one man can shake up a town just by being there and setting quiet and minding his own business, which is all ole Sly was a-doing. 'Course, he had chose his way of living, and them was the results he got from it.

Anyhow, just as ole Sly had done had enough time to get over there where he was a-going, here come Peester back in. He musta been watching and a-waiting for a chance to get at me without Sly being there. He come a-stomping over to me where I was a-setting, and he set down right across from me and planted his elbows on the table and give me his hardest look. Well, it never made me shake and tremble, the silly little ass. I just looked him back in the eyes and said, "Peester, what the hell do you want now?"

"I want that man out of town," he said. "I want him out now."

"Is that you the little ass a-talking," I asked him, "or is it the mayor?"

"Barjack," he said, "I'm serious."

"So am I," I said. " 'Cause if you're a-talking at me as a individual citizen of this here town, my answer to you is that there ain't nothing I can do about it. This here is a free country last I heard, and if a man ain't wanted by the law, and he stops by in your town and don't break no laws, then you got to put up with him a-being there. This here is the U.S.A. of America. It ain't Poland or some damn place. So shut your yap about it."

"Barjack," he said.

"On the other hand," I said, "if you're a-yapping at me as the mayor, I got even more to say. As the mayor, you got to be be aware of the laws of this here town, and you had ought to be a-setting here by my side and telling all the folks just the same thing as what I just told you. You're the most important man, even more than me, to be talking about the law. So if you personal want Sly outa town, then that's a thing between you and Sly—personal, and you had your chance to tell him about it, and you never tuck it. You went outa here like a kicked dog with your tail tucked between your legs and a-whimpering all the way out. Now I'm a-going to tell you something. I don't want to hear no more about it. Shut up. Either have a drink or get out."

"I'll have a drink," he said.

I waved at ole Aubrey, and he brung a drink over to Peester. He knowed already what Peester liked to drink. He set it down on the table and went on back to the bar. Peester gulped it down right quick and poured hisself another. I could tell that the presence of Sly in Asininity had ole Peester somewhat discombobulated, and a thought come into my head. Prob'ly I should ought to of kept it to myself, but I couldn't hardly resist the chance to job ole Peester a little bit more.

"You got someone out there what might be a-wanting to get you killed?" I asked him. "Is that how come Sly being here got you so shaky? You thinking that maybe someone paid him to blow your ass away?" He stammered a bit, and so I just went on. "You ain't got nothing to worry about, Mister Mayor, on account of ole Sly, he never does commit no murder. He prods a man into going for a gun so that he can claim self-defense whenever he final kills him. So if it is you he come after, just don't make no sudden moves whenever he gets to picking on you, calling you names and such. If he calls you a yellow-bellied, slime-sucking, goat-faced chicken, why, hell, you just smile and stay calm. That's all."

"Barjack, you son of a bitch," he said, and he was trembling mad.

"Better yet," I said, "you could just tell him that he's absolute right about all that, and that there ain't nothing you can do about it since you was born that way. Thataway you'd not only keep him from killing you, you'd be a-telling the whole truth."

Peester turned down his second drink and shoved his chair back real fast. He stood up and turned and headed for the door, and as he was a-going through it, he like to of run over ole Happy Bonapart, who was just a-coming in. Happy stepped aside and looked after the mayor for a bit. Then he come strolling on over to where I was a-setting and he plopped hisself down.

"What's wrong with the mayor?" he asked me.

"Something wrong with him?" I said. "I never noticed nothing outa the ordinary."

"Where's Sly?" Happy said.

"Likely that ain't none of your business," I said. "You got some kinda complaint against him or something?"

"Naw," he said. "I was just asking. That's all. Where's Bonnie?"

"You got anything to say that ain't a damn worthless question?" I said. "Get yourself a drink and don't say nothing more till you can think of something to say that ain't a stupid question."

Ole Happy got a pout set on his face, and he got up and walked over to the bar. He ordered hisself a drink, and whenever he got it, he brung it back to the table with him and set down. He didn't say nothing, though. He just set there a-sipping his drink. I emptied my own glass and poured me another.

"Barjack," he said of a sudden, "has you noticed? Bonnie ain't here in the room."

The little son of a bitch was smarter than what I'd been a-giving him credit for. It weren't no question. "I hadn't been a-paying no attention," I said. "You wanting

Bonnie? You wanting to take her upstairs for a little romp, are you? 'Cause if that's what it is, why, hell, I reckon we could chase her down."

"No," he said, and he said it real quick-like, like he was a-trying to shut me up. "That ain't it. I just didn't see her is all, and I was a-wondering."

"Well, I don't know where she's at," I said, "and I don't know where Sly is at, and what's more, I don't give a damn about neither one of them. It's a-getting late, and I'm headed for the house. You keep a eye on things."

"Yes sir," he said, and I got up and headed for the door. I was a little pissed off, and I couldn't figger out just exactly why, but I kinda smashed my way through the doors and stalked on over toward the White Owl. It was near time for Lillian to be closing up the place, and I meant to walk her home like I done the night before, but I figgered this night I'd go on and stay home for the night. I figgered that for a change I might even do a little romping with my sweet wife. I had just stepped offa the walkway into the street when I looked up, and I seen ole Sly step outa the White Owl along with Lillian. I stepped back into the shadders.

Lillian locked the door, and then she turned and kinda looked up at Sly. He offered his arm, and they commenced to walking down the street together. They was headed for the house. I walked along for a spell a-watching, and then I slunk along keeping a eye on them. Sure enough, ole Sly walked Lillian all the way to the house, and he stood there while she opened the door and went inside. Whenever she was safe inside and shut the door, he turned around and headed back towards downtown. I hid myself out real good, and whenever he walked right by me, I thought to myself, I could slip out my trusty ole Merwin and Hulbert Company revolver and put one lead slug right in his back and kill him dead.

Hell, no one would ever know who it was what done it, and even if they was to find out, no one wouldn't press no charges on me. Likely they'd give me a god-damn medal. Make me a big hero or something. Then I got to thinking, if I was to kill ole Sly and the word was to get out, I'd have ever' gunnie in the country a-looking for me a-trying to build up his own reputation. I sure didn't want that, and besides that, I was really getting to where I kinda liked the son of a bitch. And he hadn't gone on into the house with Lillian. He'd only walked her home was all. I let him get well on past me, and then I went on up to the house and went inside. Horace's wife Myrtle, the woman what watched our kid during the day, was done gone by then, so it was just only my little happy family there in the house. The kid come a-running at me and hollering, "Daddy."

"Ain't it your bedtime?" I said.

Lillian tuck him and went into another room with him. I found myself a bottle and a tumbler and poured myself a drink. Then I plopped down on the divan and stuck my feet up on the table there in front of it and tuck me a good swaller of the good stuff. By the time I had finished that drink, Lillian come back out. She had put the kid to bed.

"At least you could say hello to him," she said. "He's just a little boy, and he's your son."

"He's more yours than mine," I said. "You've spoiled him rotten, and I can't stand him."

"That's an awful thing for you to say, Barjack," she said. "Why did you even bother coming home? Why didn't you just stay with your whore again?" Well, there, she had done went and said it.

"Bonnie Boodle's my business partner," I said. "Me and her—"

"Don't tell me any lies, Barjack," she said. "I know what goes on. If you think you're fooling me, you're even more stupid than I thought."

"Well, I seen what you done tonight," I said. "I seen you walking home a-snuggling with that killer."

"Mr. Sly is a perfect gentleman," she said. "You weren't there, so he walked me home, and if you were spying on us, you know that's all there was to it."

"I bet it weren't all you were thinking about," I said. "Nor him, neither."

"If anyone was thinking thoughts like that," she said, "no one gave voice to them."

"Well, la dee da," I said, and I poured myself another drink. Lillian turned and headed for our bedroom. She slammed the door behind her. I drunk myself another tumbler full, and then I got to thinking about her in there in that big bed, and I got to recalling all her female charms and curves what had trapped me into this situation in the first place, as well as the reason I had told myself I was a-coming on home that night. I pulled off my boots and throwed them on the floor. Then I stood up and tuck off my coat and vest and my gun belt. I throwed them all on the divan, and then I throwed my shirt and my trousers on there with them. I puffed myself up and walked into the bedroom a-grinning. Lillian set up straight, a-pulling the sheet up under her chin.

"Barjack," she said.

"Hell," I said, "let's make up."

"You get out of here," she said.

"It's my goddamned bed," I said.

"Well, you're not sleeping in it," she said. "Not with me."

"Aw, come on, Lillian," I said, and I tuck another couple steps toward her. She reached over to the little table there beside the bed, and I be damned straight to hell if she didn't come out with a little snub-nosed revolver of some kind, and she thumbed back the hammer and aimed that little squirty son of a bitch right at me.

"Get out," she said.

"Now, Lillian," I said.

"Get out of here, Barjack," she said, "or I'll kill you."

I turned to run just as she pulled the trigger, and the damned bullet nicked my left ear. I yelped like a kicked dog and run for the front door. I run hard into it 'cause I fumbled with the door handle, but then I got it open and tuck out. Lillian had got outa bed and follered me. She stood in the doorway and fired another round as I was a-running across the way there a-headed back for the main street of the town. Just then I learnt how tender my feet was on accounta stepping on sharp rocks and stickers and things, and I was a-running and a-hopping and yowling all the way back to the Hooch House.

Whenever I run in through the front door, ever'one in there set up straight and stared with their eyes opened real wide. I just straightened myself up real proud-like and walked through that big room over to the stairs and on up, and I went into Bonnie's room. Happy was in there a-humping her. I set down in a chair. "Don't mind me," I said. Bonnie pulled the sheet up clean over their heads, and I just set there a-waiting for them to get the job done. In another minute or two, ole Happy come out from under that sheet, and his face was bright red. He tried to keep hisself covered up with the sheet while he pulled his britches back on, and he never looked at me, not straight. He got hisself dressed and hurried out the door.

Bonnie set up and give me a hard look. Her great big titties was hanging down full exposed.

"How was he?" I said.

"He was just fine till you come in," she said.

"Whyn't you lock the damn door?" I said.

"I will from now on," she said. "What's wrong with you?"

"Aw, hell," I said, "I'm all right. Lillian tuck a shot at me is all. I had to run for my life just the way you see me here."

"It looks like she hit you," Bonnie said.

"She just only nicked my ear is all," I said. "Ears bleed like hell. It ain't nothing."

"It's a good thing she ain't much of a shot," said Bonnie.

"It'd be tough for me to hit a moving target with that little snub-nosed son of a bitch she was a-using," I said.

Just then Bonnie throwed the sheet clean off and come stark nekkid outa the bed. She flounced her big floppy body over to the door and jerked it open. "Aubrey," she yelled out. God, she had a awful voice whenever she yelled like that. Then she looked over her shoulder at me. "Take the rest of them clothes off," she said.

Well, before long she had me a bath fixed up there

and had me a-setting in it. I was puffing me a good cigar and had me a tumbler of whiskey in my hand, and ole Bonnie, she was a-washing me all over. That was after she had already washed up my bloody ear and put some kinda salve on it. She had scrubbed me in ever' place imaginable, and I was still a-smoking and a-drinking, but I was getting some aroused from all that activity, and then, damned if she didn't step over the edge and drop her fat ass down in that sudsy water with me. A bunch of water sloshed over the edge of the tub when she settled herself down, and I scooted back as much as I could, 'cause the two of us more than filled up that little tub.

"Damn, Bonnie," I said, "you're going to flood the Hooch House."

"Let them swim," she said, and she wriggled around and commenced to fondling on me, so I put my cigar down and my tumbler, and I reached my arms around her as far as I could and give her a big wet smooch. We fooled around like that for a bit, and then she washed her own self up some, and we got out and she dried us off. Then she tuck a hold of me by the handle and pulled me towards the bed. "Come on, Barjack," she said. I didn't have no choice. I had to foller her or lose it, so pretty quick we was in that bed a-getting after it.

When we was all done and laid back and relaxing, ole Bonnie throwed a arm over my chest and kinda nuzzled me. "She really try to kill you?" she asked me.

"She said she would," I told her. "Then she shot my ear, and when I was a-running away from the house, she tuck one more shot at me. That's all I know."

"You and me're real good together," she said. "Ain't we?"

"There's never been no better," I said.

"I wouldn'ta had Happy nor no one else up here like that," she said, "except for you taken to walking your wife home again."

"Forget it, Bonnie," I said. "Hell, it don't matter no more."

"You ain't mad?" she said.

"Hell, no," I said. "I ain't mad."

"You know, Barjack," she said, but I never let her finish what she was fixing to say.

"I know," I said. "I made a hell of a mistake whenever I married that woman. She charmed me like a goddamn witch woman or something. She trapped me into it, and now there ain't no way out. It's all true, and I know it, and I don't want no more talk about it."

"All right," she said, "but from now on, why don't you just stay right here? Leave her with the house and the White Owl. You and me'll be just fine here at the Hooch House. This is our kinda place anyhow, Barjack. You and me're right at home here."

I didn't give her no answer just then, but I was thinking that she couldn'ta been no more right about that. Besides, if I was to go back to the house, ole Lillian might get off a better shot the next time. I give ole Bonnie a sloppy kiss, and then I said, "Someone'll have to go get my clothes and my guns."

"I'll take care of that tomorrow while she's at the White Owl," Bonnie said.

"You do that for me, Bonnie, ole gal," I said. "You know, I been thinking about what you said a bit ago."

"Yeah?" she said. "What's that?"

"About me just staying here," I said. "I think that's a

hell of a good idee, and I'm thinking that I might just do that."

"Oh, Barjack," she said, and she flung herself on me and mashed her lips against mine and like to smothered me to death before she let up. Then she said, "You want me to pour you a drink, baby?"

Chapter Five

I was having my breakfast of eggs and whiskey in the Hooch House the next morning whenever ole Happy come a-running in like as if Jesse James and his gang was a-headed for the bank. "Barjack," he hollered, "come quick! There's big trouble!"

"What the hell are you talking about?" I said.

"Sam Hooper and Silver Spike Hanlon," he said. "They're a-fixing to shoot it out right out there on the street."

"Oh, hell," I said. I jerked the napkin out from under my chin and throwed it down hard right on top of my plate of food, which was only just about half et, and I stood up fast and knocked my chair over backwards. "Goddamn it," I said. "Can't a man have a breakfast in peace around this here town?"

"Someone's going to get killed, Barjack," Happy said.

"Well, whyn't you stop them?" I asked him on my way to the door.

"I tried," Happy said, "but ole Silver Spike aimed a six-gun at me and told me to mind my own business."

We both hit the door about the same time, and I had to shove Happy outa the way so I could get through it. He follered me on outside. I stopped on the sidewalk and looked down the street. I seen Sam Hooper first. He was standing on the boardwalk just in front of the White Owl, and he was holding a gun down at his side. I looked down the street where he seemed to be a-looking, and sure enough, there was ole Silver Spike Hanlon, and he was a-holding a shooter in his hand, too. There was four cowhands on horses back behind ole Silver Spike. I walked out in the middle of the street, kinda right between the two of them. I hitched my britches up over my belly and harrumphed real loud.

"Hold ever'thing here," I called out. "What the hell is this all about?"

"The son of a bitch hired a killer to get me," Silver Spike said. "I come to get him first. It's a matter of self-defense. You just stay out of it, Barjack. It's between me and Hooper. It ain't got nothing to do with the law."

"If you're a-fixing to discharge firearms on the street of my town," I said, "then I reckon it's the law's business, and by God, it's mine."

"It's five against one," Hooper yelled from over in front of the White Owl. "He can't even fight me fair. Besides, I never sent for Sly. He done it, 'cause he's afraid to fight me fair."

"What about them four cowboys?" I said to ole Silver Spike.

He looked over his shoulder at the boys a-setting horseback.

"I don't need them," he said. "They just come in with me 'cause I didn't know how many Hooper was bringing along with him. You boys can ride on back to the ranch." The four cowhands hesitated a bit, and then Silver Spike said, "Go on now. I mean it. You want ever'one in town to think I'm a-skeered of Sam Hooper? Go on."

The four turned their horses and rode on out. Ever'one was quiet and just stood there a-watching till they was well gone. Then I figgered it was time for me to take charge again. "Come on out here, boys," I said. "Come on over here to me." The both of them just kinda looked at me and then looked back at each other. "Goddamn it," I yelled, "holster them six-guns and walk over here."

It tuck a minute of thinking on his part, but final ole Hooper shoved his gun in the holster and commenced to moving slowly toward me. Silver Spike waited even longer, but then he done the same thing. They come up one on each side of me, but they never looked at me. They was a-staring hard at each other, and I could see a killing mood in both of their faces.

"You ain't going to stop this, Barjack," Hooper said. "That son of a bitch has been wanting to kill me for nigh onto fifteen years."

"But I ain't never took a shot at you, have I?" Silver Spike said. "I never gave you no call to bring in a professional killer."

"I never did," Hooper said. "You keep saying that so Barjack won't believe that it was you that hired him, which you did."

"Shut the hell up, the both of you," I said. "Each one

of you keeps accusing the other'n of bringing in the Widdermaker. Did it ever come into your brains through your thick skulls that maybe neither one of you done it? Hell, ole Rumproast come in here the other day and got hisself shot and throwed in jail 'cause he was so sure that Sly come after him. He couldn'ta come after ever'one. And he told me he didn't come after no one. He come for a rest and that's all."

"He would say that," Silver Spike said.

"Now, I want the both of you to turn around and get on your horses and ride on outa town," I said. They never moved. "I mean it," I said. "Right now."

"If I turn around," Hooper said, "Silver Spike'll shoot me in the back."

"He says that 'cause he knows that's what he's planning to do to me," Silver Spike said.

Outa the corner of my eye I seen ole Happy sneaking up on the blind side of them two ornery cusses, and he was a-carrying a shotgun. I was sure glad to see him, and I was hoping he'd get close enough to use it before either one of them old bastards was to try something.

"There ain't nothing I can say to get you to call this here thing off?" I asked.

"We'll call it off after one of us is dead," Hooper said.

"All right, then," I said. "Let me have your guns."

I held out my hand right in between them and waited, but neither one of the two old farts made no move. Happy come up closer, and he pointed that greener in the general direction of the three of us. I hoped that it never occured to Hooper and Hanlon that if Happy was to for real shoot that thing, he'd kill all three of us. And I hoped that Happy was aware of that simple fact too.

"Unbuckle your belts," he said out loud.

They looked over and seen Happy with that scattergun aimed in their direction, and then they started in to unbuckling. Hanlon got his off first and handed it over to me. "That was a dirty trick, Barjack," he said. Then Hooper handed me his. I throwed the belts over my shoulder, and I turned to walk up on the sidewalk.

"Have at it now, you two old bastards," I said. "Go on. Happy, grab us a couple of chairs over there. We'll set and watch."

"What do you mean?" Hooper said.

Me and ole Happy tuck us our seats there in front of the general store and leaned them back against the wall. Happy kept that shotgun across his knees.

"You two come in here to fight," I said. "So fight."

They looked at each other, and they looked at me. I never seen two such stupid-looking old men before in my whole entire damn life.

"You mean, just start slugging?" Hooper said.

"Slugging, kicking, biting," I said. "I don't give a damn, so long as you ain't shooting. Oh, yeah, no knives neither."

"How about clubs?" Happy said.

"Hell, if one of them can get ahold of one, let him use it," I said. "Well, hell, boys, we're a-waiting."

By this time quite a little crowd had gethered up along both sides of the street to see what was going on, and the two old bastards was getting more than a little embarrassed. Ole Peester come a-walking up to me just then.

"What's this all about, Barjack?" he said.

"Not much," I said. "These two old relics here come

into town a-wanting to kill each other, but I tuck away their guns. Now they won't fight. I think they're really a-skeered of each other."

"I ain't scared of him," Hooper said, looking over at me. "I just ain't going to take the first swing, that's all."

Just then ole Silver Spike swung a wild right and caught Hooper alongside the jaw, and ole Hooper staggered back a few steps and fell back on his ass a-setting up. He set there a few seconds a-rubbing his jaw. Then he managed to get up onto his feet, and he doubled up his both fists and started stepping in toward Silver Spike.

"Try that again, you coward," he said. "I wasn't looking. Try it again."

Ole Sam Hooper started in to dancing around Silver Spike Hanlon, and Silver Spike was a-turning to foller him, and for a spell the two ole farts just kinda danced around with each other like that. Then one of them, I can't recall just which one, or maybe I never really could tell in the first place, but one of them throwed a punch, and then the two of them was swinging with both fists as fast as they could. The trouble was, neither one of them landed on nothing but the other'n's arms and shoulders. Even so, pretty soon they was both red in the face and and a-puffing real hard. Then they kinda backed off and stood panting and staring at the ground.

"You two had enough?" I called out to them. Ole Silver Spike shot me a mean and dirty look.

"Hell no," he said. "I'm just taking a breather."

Sam Hooper tuck advantage of Silver Spike a-looking over at me, and he driv a hard right into ole Silver Spike's belly. Silver Spike doubled over with a loud *whoof,* and he just stood there like that, his knees bent a little and leaning way over at the waist a-looking at the ground between his feet. Someone out in the crowd yelled out, "Finish him off, Sam," but Sam never. He just stood there a-looking at ole Silver Spike bent double.

Just then ole Herman Sly come a-walking outa the White Owl. He seen the crowd a-gethered around there, and then he seen the two old men in the street. He figgered out what was up, all right. He stepped down offa the board sidewalk and walked across the street behind ole Sam Hooper's back and come on over to where I was a-setting with Happy Bonapart, and Happy still with that shotgun laying across his knees.

"Marshal Barjack," he said by way of greeting.

"Howdy there, Mister Sly," I said.

"What's all this about," he said, "if I may ask?"

"I reckon you may," I said. "It's just two old goddamned fools what has hated each other for fifteen years, and now that you're in town, why, each one swears the other'n sent for you to do him in. They come into town to shoot each other, but I tuck away their irons and made them duke it out, as you see here."

"You probably made a wise decision, Marshal," he said. "I'm sorry to be the cause of so much trouble in your town. This sort of thing happens almost anywhere I stop. Excuse me."

He touched the brim of his hat and walked on into the Hooch House.

"Well, I be damned," I said.

"What?" Happy said.

"He ain't even sticking around to watch the fight what he hisself is the cause of," I said. "You ever know of a man to walk away from a fight like that?"

"They ain't much fighting going on right now," Happy said, and I looked back out in the street, and he was right as rain. Ole Silver Spike had just straightened hisself up and was kinda stretching and holding his sides and sucking in air real deep-like. Whenever he straightened hisself, ole Sam Hooper put up his dukes again and commenced to dancing some more. That one punch had give his confidence a hell of a boost.

"Come on," he said. "Come on."

Well, they started in their wild swinging again, doing about as much damage as they had did before, mostly, 'course, to their lungs, but ole Silver Spike, he seemed to be doing the most damage, meaning only that he was a-making Sam Hooper back up a little bit. But you know, once a feller starts into backing, it's damn difficult to stop it. Ole Sam, he kept on a-swinging, but he also kept on a-backing, and the more he backed the faster ole Silver Spike come forward at him. The next thing you know, ole Sam had backed right into a watering trough, and whenever he done that, why, he just natural-like tumbled over backwards into it, and ole Silver Spike was a-moving so hard and fast into Sam that he went on in on top of Sam.

Well, there was a mighty splash, and the crowd give a hoot and a holler and commenced to hoorawing something crazy. In that trough, what seemed kinda little now with them two big bastards a-floundering around in it, Sam and Silver Spike was all tangled together. They flapped their arms and legs around, a-trying to get loose from one another and trying to get up outa the trough, and they was a-spitting and a-spluttering like someone what had fell into the middle of the river off the side of a damned ole riverboat.

Final, ole Silver Spike managed to get his ass outa the trough, and right after that Sam heaved his own self out. The two of them was standing there a-dripping and a-trying to shake water off theirselves, and the crowd was laughing like hell. Just as the laughing kinda died down a bit, someone out there yelled out, "That's the first bath ole Sam Hooper's had in a year," and the roar went up again. I got up and I said to Happy, "Bring them two assholes into the Hooch House." I went on inside to wait.

I picked out a different table from what I had been at before, 'cause I seen right away that ole Aubrey had never bothered to pick up my breakfast plate. I got my bottle and tumbler offa the table first, though, and when Happy come in with the two still-dripping-wet combatants, I was setting there a-sipping whiskey. I waved them on over to my table. Both fighters was a-hanging their wet heads and looking kinda shamefaced. "Happy," I said, "go get three more glasses." Happy headed for the bar, and I said, "Set down."

They set with a empty chair between them, and neither one of them looked up at me. I just let them set there quiet-like till Happy come back. Then I poured four drinks, and I shoved them all around the table. Happy said, "Thanks, Barjack."

"Shut up," I said. Then, to them two old fools, I said, "Drink up. It's on the town of Asininity."

They each picked up a glass and tuck a sip.

"Take a good swaller," I said, and they did. "Now," I said, "how do you feel?"

Neither one give me a answer.

"Do you feel any better now that you've fit?" I said. "Hell, you been wanting to do that for fifteen years, ain't you? So do you feel any better?"

I tuck me another drink a-waiting for an answer, but I still never got none. I said, "Just what was it started this here fight in the first place?"

"You made us do it, Barjack," Sam said.

"Hell," I said, "I don't mean just now. I mean fifteen year ago. What started it?"

I swear to God, them two old farts was just like a mirror image. Right at the exact same time they turned and pointed a finger at the other'n and said right together, "He did."

"Damn it," I said. "I didn't ask you who started it. I asked you what started it. What was it all over?"

"Well," said Sam, but he never got no further.

"Well, he went and . . . ," said Silver Spike, but he kinda got stuck for words, too.

"You don't even know no more, do you?" I said. "Neither one of you?"

"They don't know?" Happy said.

"Shut up, Happy," I said. I drank up the rest of the whiskey what was in my glass, and then I told the others, "Drink up," and they did, and I poured another round. Well, I kept on like that for a while, a-talking and a-belittling them two and a-drinking and a-pouring drinks all around, and by and by I had the both of them wobbly-legged drunk. Ole Happy, too. Then I looked around till I seen ole Sly a-setting off by hisself a-drinking coffee, and I waved him over. He stood up and come over to where we was at.

"You want me, Marshal?" he asked.

"That's how come me to wave at you," I said. "Mister Sly, I reckon it might could be a violation of your professional ethics or code or something, but I want to ask you a question, and I would appreciate it a whole hell of a lot if you was to give me a straight and honest answer right here in front of these two silly ole sons a bitches. Would you do that for me, do you reckon?"

"I don't know that until I hear the question, Marshal," Sly said, "but I will promise you this much. If I give you an answer at all, it will be a truthful one."

"Well, I'll just have to settle for that, I reckon," I said. "Now here's the question." I turned on the two fighters. "I want you two to pay attention to this here, too. Now, Mister Sly," I went on, "did you, sir, come to town with the intent of killing either one of these two old fools?"

"Marshal," he said, "I did not."

"Thank you, sir," I said, and Sly went back to his coffee. "Now, are you two satisfied with that?" I asked.

"I, um, I guess so," Hooper said final.

"I s'pose I was wrong about that Sly," Silver Spike said.

"All right, then," I said. "Now how about this here fifteen-year-long feud?"

"What do you mean?" Silver Spike said.

"Now that you seen how damn foolish you are, the both of you," I said, "you willing to call this here thing off? I ain't going to ask you to shake hands nor nothing that cozy. I know that'd be asking too much. Just are you willing to call off your damn feud?"

Them two looked up at each other real slow, and then they looked over at me.

"I guess so," said Hooper.

"Yeah," said Silver Spike.

"Well, by God, that's something good come outa all this," I said, and I poured another round. Just then ole Rod Corley come a-hustling into the Hooch House. He was one of Silver Spike's cowhands. He looked around and spied his boss and come a-running over.

"Mister Hanlon," he said. "I got to see you right away."

"Well, I'm right here, Rod," Silver Spike said. "What is it?"

Ole Rod, he looked kinda sheepish at me and then at Hooper. "It's Billy," he said.

"Well?" Silver Spike said. "What about him?"

"He's been killed, Mister Hanlon," Rod said.

Ole Silver Spike's face went kinda white, and he looked up at Rod.

"How?" he said.

Rod looked back at Hooper.

"Well, sir," he said.

"Come on," said Silver Spike. "Out with it."

"It was Davey Cline," said Rod. "One of Mister Hooper's hands. He shot him."

Chapter Six

Well, I figgered that would for sure blow the lid offa ever'thing right then and there, and all my hard work was fixing to go for nothing. I figgered them two old bastards would commence to killing one another again right there in front a me and ole Happy and even the Undertaker hisself a-setting back against the wall a-watching. I figgered—But, hell, it never happened. The two old feudists both just looked real tired and real sad. I stood on up with a sigh and hitched my britches.

"Where's Davey at?" I said.

Hooper spoke up right quick before ole Rod could answer me. "Barjack," he said, "let me bring him in. I can bring him in without no trouble. It's my fault this thing has happened."

"Yours and mine," Silver Spike said. "Let him do it, Barjack."

"Well," I said, acting like as if it was a real tough decision for me to make, but actual I didn't want to go running off on no manhunt nohow, "I'll give you till this time tomorrer, Sam. If you ain't brung him in by then, I'll have to go out after him with a posse."

"Thanks," said Hooper. "I'll bring him back, I promise you." I handed him his gun belt. He tuck it and strapped it on. "I hope I won't need this," he said. Then he looked at ole Rod. "Come on," he said. "You show me where it happened."

Rod looked at his boss, and Silver Spike got up too. I noticed that spike of hair a-sticking out on the right-hand side of his head. Funny, I hadn't really noticed it since all his hair had turned white some years ago, but when he was still a young man, the spike had been white and the rest of his hair was brown. That's how he come to have that name. I handed him his iron. "I got to go take care of Billy," he said. Then, to Hooper, he added, "I'll ride along with you that far, if you don't mind my company."

"You're welcome," Hooper said. "We'll all ride together."

I watched them all walk outa there in a bunch, and then I heaved up a heavy sigh. "Goddamn," I said, "I hope them two ole farts ain't fooling me none about all this. I hope they really have seen the damn foolishness of their ways and has made it up once and for all. Otherwise I might a just got someone else killed by sending them all out together like that with all their damn guns."

"I think they meant what they said, Barjack," said Happy. "It'll be all right."

"Hell, Happy, how would you know?" I said. I poured

me a fresh tumbler of whiskey and tuck me a big gulp. "I hope you're right," I said. Of usual I was kinda rough on ole Happy, but for once, it come to me that I shouldn'ta said to him what I had just said.

Well, it was still kinda early in the day, and them two old farts and their damn fool fight had caused me to already drink a little bit more whiskey than what I usual drunk by that time of day. To tell you the whole damn truth, I was beginning to feel just a bit woozy. I decided that maybe what I needed in order to face the rest of the day with any kinda equilibrium and dignity was just a little nap, so I got myself up. "I'm going upstairs for a little while, Happy," I said. "Try not to bother me for nothing what comes up. Okay?"

"Okay, Barjack," Happy said. "I'll handle things."

A cowboy come a-walking down the stairs with a silly grin on his face, and I reckoned I knowed what he'd been a-doing up there. I passed him by and started to making my own way up there. I was just about halfway whenever ole Bonnie come a-flouncing her way down. When the two of us was about to pass each other by, I reached out my arm across her big titties and grabbed onto her opposite-side shoulder. "Come on," I said, and I turned her right around there on the stairs and tuck her on along with me back up to her room.

We got us in there, and I just went right over to the bed and flopped down hard on my back, a-bouncing the bed and squeaking the springs. "Come here, Bonnie," I said, and she come over and set on the bed by me. I pulled her right on down beside me, and then I used her big titties for a piller to lay my weary and dizzy head on. "I just need me some rest," I said. "Just for a little while. That's all."

"And you want me with you just for that?" Bonnie said.

"Yeah," I said. "I do." At that she put a arm right around me and hugged me tight, and then I said, "Bonnie, did you just now have that cowboy up here? The one I just seen going downstairs?"

"Yeah," she said. "What of it?"

"Nothing," I said. "I ain't going to make nothing out of it, nor nothing else you ever done before right now. Not even whenever you tried to kill me that one time."

"Which time was that?" she asked me.

"Never mind," I said. "But I been thinking, Bonnie. Since I went and made up my mind to stay over here with you and not go home to Lillian no more, you know, I'd like it better if you didn't take on no customers no more. You know what I mean?"

She squealed a little and squeezed me tight again, and she said in her littlest voice, "Yeah, Barjack. I know. From now it'll just be you and me." Well, I went to sleep on her then, and I slept real good.

Whenever I final woke up again I was hungry as hell. It was some after noon by then, and as you might recall from what all had transpired at nearly the break of day, I hadn't got to eat up my whole breakfast that morning. I set on up, and ole Bonnie, she kinda moaned a little like as if she been a-sleeping too. She stretched around some, and her flesh wiggled all over, and then the both of us set up on opposite sides of the bed. I yawned real wide and loud. "You get enough sleep, honey?" she said.

"Yeah," I said. "I did, but I could eat a whole damn horse right now. Not a little saddle horse, neither. One of them great big wagon-pulling bastards."

"I'll just run on downstairs and get Aubrey to cooking you up a steak and taters," she said.

"Okay, darlin'," I said, "but don't run, just walk. I ain't in such a hurry that I want you to go falling down no stairs. I'll come a-crawling along behind you in just a minute or so."

Bonnie left the room, and then I seen that someone had pulled my gunbelt and my boots offa me while I was a-sleeping. It had to been Bonnie, but whenever I had went to sleep I was laying on her titties and when I woke up I was still there. She had to done some fancy maneuvering to keep from waking me up to do all that. Either that or else I was damn near dead to the world, and someone coulda carried me off and hanged me till I woke up dead. Anyhow, I shuck my head to clear it, pulled my boots on, stood up, and strapped my six-gun back on. I noticed that I had to hook that belt buckle up to the very last hole. I didn't have much room left for gaining no more weight. I hitched my britches and headed out the door and down the hall.

At the top of the stairs I could see the whole big room down below. Ole Sly, the Widowmaker, was still just a-setting there in his favorite place. Either that or else he'd gone out and come back while I was sleeping. There was four or five cowhands setting around a table, and ole Happy was standing at the bar beside Bonnie. I didn't see Aubrey nowhere, so I figgered that Bonnie had done sent him back to the kitchen to cook up my steak. I lumbered on down the stairs.

I didn't feel like bellying up to the bar, so I headed myself for a table, but before I could set my lard ass down, ole Sly kinda beckoned to me with his gun hand. "Would you care to join me, Marshal?" he said. I went on over there and set with him.

"I don't mind," I said.

"You've had a full day already," he said, "and I think it's all because of me. I regret that. Believe me."

"I reckon your presence in this here town had a little something to do with it," I said, "but I can't see it being your fault. Them two, Hooper and Hanlon, has been after each other's ass for fifteen year now, and they can't neither one of them even remember what the hell got it all started in the first damn place. All you done was just bring it to a head, you know, aggravate it a little, and that was bound to happen sooner or later anyhow. Besides, when it was all over with, it got them to call off the feud. If you want to take the blame for the fight, then you got to take credit for the finish of it, too."

"That much is well and good," Sly said, "but it's not the whole story. A man has been killed over it, after all."

"If them thickheaded young cowhands wants to go taking potshots at each other on account of the argument between their bosses," I said, "then they just gets what they deserves. That's how I see it. Hell, Sly, if I actual and for real thought that you was to blame for the unfortunate killing of young Billy Duvall, I'd slap your ass in a jail cell or at least run you outa town, and I got no intention of doing neither one of them things."

"I'm glad to hear that," he said. "I'd hate to have to face you, Barjack."

I wondered just how he meant that, 'cause I knowed

for sure that I wouldn't never stand face-to-face with the Widowmaker, not making no challenge. I might shoot him in the back or hit him in the back of the head with a two-by-four or something. Then I thought that maybe he somehow knowed that about me and that was how come he said what he said. Bonnie come over just then, and kinda put a end to my musings. She was a-carrying my bottle and tumbler. She give me a real sweet look. "You want this, honey babe?" she said.

"Yeah," I said. "Set down, Bonnie."

She set beside me and poured me out a drink. Then she hugged my near arm with both of hers and smiled into my face. It kinda embarrassed me, but I decided to let it go. "Maybe Mister Sly here would like one of them steaks," I said. "Did you ask him?"

"No, thank you," he said. "I had my lunch across the street."

"Oh," I said, and I wondered how him and my Lillian was getting on. Then I caught myself on that one. She weren't really my Lillian no more. She had run me off a-shooting at me to kill me, and I had done told Bonnie that I meant to stay with her and not never go back home no more. It really weren't none of my business how ole Lillian was a-doing with Sly nor with no one else. I decided that I would have to get that notion set firm in my mind. I was hitched up to her firm and legal, but that was all. I figgered that maybe one of these days, I'd have to see if there weren't some way of dealing with that annoying little problem. I tuck me a drink, and in another minute ole Aubrey brung me my plate. He checked on Sly's coffee, went for the pot, and brung him a refill. I tied into that food on my plate and didn't say nothing more till I was done eating.

I did just happen to notice out of the corner of my right eye little ole Chester Filbert, the clerk over at the dry goods store, come a-fidgeting into the bar. I was some surprised at that, 'cause Chester didn't hardly ever come in, but I was too busy eating, and Chester was too damned insignificant to worry my head with. Then I seen Chester kinda lean across the bar and say something real low to ole Aubrey. Then he actual had hisself a drink. One drink, and then he left. By and by, Aubrey come back to the table to check on us.

"What was ole Chester a-whispering to you about?" I asked him.

"Well," Aubrey said, "oh, it was nothing."

I seen, though, that he give a look at Sly while he was a-saying that, and I figgered he was lying to me. "What the hell did the little son of a bitch say, Aubrey?" I said, with my voice a little more forceful and demanding-like.

"He asked me how long Mister Sly here is going to be in town," Aubrey said.

I looked at Sly then, and he was a-eyeballing me at the same time. "What'd you tell him?" I asked Aubrey.

Aubrey shrugged. "Told him I didn't know," he said.

"All right," I said, dismissing ole Aubrey. He went on back over to the bar, and went to swiping at it with a dirty rag.

"Another one," Sly said.

"Chester?" I said. "Hell, he couldn'ta done nothing to make a man want to pay real money just to have him get killed. Anyone wanted Chester dead would just swat him like a fly. He's just nervous, ole Chester, that's all. A running horse makes him nervous. A barking dog, even."

"Well, maybe you're right, Marshal," Sly said. "I hope so."

We set there a-jawing like that some more for a spell, and then I got me a real big surprise. In come Hooper, Hanlon, Rod Corley, and Davey Cline, big as you please. And ever' damn one of them had his six-guns strapped on, even ole Davey hisself. They come a-walking over to the table where we was a-setting. I stood up to meet them, ready for most anything that might happen.

"Let's go on over to the jailhouse, boys," I said.

"Wait just a minute, Barjack," Silver Spike said. "There's something you need to hear first."

I set back down kinda easy-like. "I'm a-listening," I said.

Then Hooper, he tuck over. "Rod here saw the whole thing," he said. "He was there when it happened."

"Go on. Tell the marshal just exactly what really happened out there, Rod," said Silver Spike.

"Well, sir," said Rod, giving a shrug and looking down at the floor, "ole Billy, he drawed first. Even got off the first shot. But he missed."

I looked at each one of them faces a-standing there around me, and I knowed damn well if I knowed anything in the whole entire world that they was lying to me, but then I knowed a couple of other things too. One was that being as how I was just only a town marshal, I didn't really have no jurisdiction over whatever it was that happened out there outside of town. And if I didn't have to mess with it, I didn't really want to be bothered none. But the main thing I knowed for sure by what was happening right there in fronta my own nose was that this here was the final proof that the long-standing Hooper and Hanlon feud was actual and forreal over with. Them two had final made up, so much so that here they was conspiring together right under my nose to cover up a murdering. I looked hard at ole Davey, the young killer, and he ducked his head to look at the floor between his boots.

"Davey," I said, "what ole Rod said, is that for sure the way it happened out there? And don't lie to me, boy."

"Yes, sir," he said. "That's the way it was, and I'm real sorry it happened."

I looked from Sam Hooper to Silver Spike Hanlon, and then I said, "Is there going to be any repercussions from this here killing? Is this damn feud fixing to reinvigorate itself?"

"It's over," said Hanlon.

"There won't be any more trouble," Hooper said. "You have our word on that."

"All right, then," I said. "I'm a taking your word. You all can go on back to your ranches."

They went on and left the place then, and I tuck me another drink of that good whiskey.

"Ain't that nice?" Bonnie said. "Why, I swear I never thought I'd see the day that them two would agree on anything."

"You believe them, Marshal?" Sly asked me.

"Yeah," I said. "I do. If they meant to keep up the feuding and fighting, they wouldn'ta even come in here."

"That's not what I meant," he said.

I give Sly a hard look then, and I said, "I know what you meant."

"Then I know what your answer is," he said.

Bonnie squinched her face up and looked at me and looked at him. "What are you two talking about?" she said.

"Nothing," I said. "Don't worry your pretty head none."

"You was talking about something," she said. "Tell me. I don't like to be talked around, and me a-setting right here listening to you like that. What was he talking about he knows what your answer was? Tell me, Barjack."

"Goddamn it," I said, "they was lying to me. All of them."

"You mean the feud's still on?" she said.

"No, sweet," I said. "The feud's off. That's for sure. They was lying about how Billy Duvall got killed. Billy never shot first. He was murdered by Davey, and that's a certain thing for sure."

"But," she stammered, "but—You let them go, Barjack."

"Number one, darlin' dear," I said, "if the only witness what seen it all says that Billy drawed and fired first, there ain't nothing I can do. Number two, if the boss of the dead man ain't wanting to press no charges, then I reckon I had oughta be satisfied, 'cause, number three, what it means is that Hanlon and Hooper has quit the feud forever, and they ain't intending for nothing to start it up again. That what it all means."

"Oh," she said, drawing it out real long-like as if things was real slow settling in on her brain.

"And then there's number four," I said.

"What's number four?" she said.

"The whole damn thing tuck place outside of my jurisdiction as marshal of this here town," I said. "Legal, there ain't nothing I could do about it nohow."

Happy Bonapart come in just then, and he come over to set with us. I asked him if he wanted a drink, but he said he never. He called to ole Aubrey for a cup of coffee, though, and it come to me that maybe he was a-trying to act like ole Sly there, and I come near to telling him that it would take a heap more than sipping coffee all day for him to ever come close to being like ole Sly, but I kept my yap shut for a change. Happy, he tuck a sip of coffee and burned his tongue.

"I just come from the jailhouse," he said. "Doc was over there taking a look at ole Rumproast. He says that Rumproast is might' near ready to go home now—that is, if you're willing to let him go."

"Give him another couple of days to really cool off," I said, and then I got to thinking about how the long-standing Hooper and Hanlon feud had come to a end that very day, and how me and ole Bonnie had us a new understanding and all that, and I tossed down what was left in my tumbler, and I said, "Aw, hell, Happy, go on back over there and tell the kid he can go on home."

I think that ole Sly actual smiled a little at that.

Chapter Seven

I noticed over the next few days that ole Sly was spending more and more time over at ole Lillian's place of business, and whenever she closed the place up at night, why, it had just become a natural and expected thing for him to walk her on home. The nights was getting a little more chillier all the time, and once I even seen him with a arm around her shoulders. But what I have to say for ole Sly is I have to say that he never so far as I knowed went inside the house. He always just only shuck her hand there at the door and said good night, and she went in, and then he walked on back to the Hooch House all by his lonesome. Like ole Lillian said, he was a real gentleman.

I was about to think that ever'thing had settled down again in Asininity in spite of the fact that the Widdermaker was in town. All the ones what had thought that he had come to town to kill them had final figgered out that it just weren't so. Like I said, I was just about a-thinking along them lines whenever ole Peester come into my office early one morning. I don't know what the hell I was a-doing in there. Usual, if I was up and around that early, I was over at the Hooch House, but for some damn reason I was in the marshaling office, and I was there by my own self. Ole Happy hadn't reported in yet. Peester come in and shut the door behind him. Then he come over to my desk like as if he had some kinda secret about him.

"What the hell's wrong with you?" I asked him.

"Barjack," he said, keeping his voice low, even though me and him was the only ones around, "when are you going to do something about Sly?"

"I thought we had done had this here conversation," I said. "Why do I got to do anything about ole Sly? What's he done?"

"One man was shot up and another killed," Peester said. "There was a brawl in the street, and it was all because of Sly being here."

"The man what got shot up, what was ole Rumproast, he come into the Hooch House and tuck a shot at Sly," I said. "Sly coulda killed him, but he never. And the one what did get killed was outa town, and the witness said that he went for his gun first, so that there was a case a self-defense, and Sly weren't nowhere near where it happened nohow. And if you're a-calling that silly fight between them two old men a brawl, why, I'd say you ain't never seen no real brawl. The only thing I can see what Sly has caused around here is he caused them two old fools to call off their fifteen-year-long feud. Now, what the hell's your problem?"

"I suppose it doesn't matter to you that Sly has been seen walking your wife home every evening," Peester said.

"Mister Mayor, you son of a bitch," I said, "you just count yourself damn lucky I don't knock the piss outa you right here, or even blow your worthless ass away deader'n hell, 'cause that ain't none of your goddamn business."

"All right, all right," he said, "but Barjack, something has got to be done. We can't have his kind just hanging around our town."

It come to me then of a sudden that ole Peester was way too worried about Sly being with us, and it just didn't make no sense to me unless, as I thought briefly before, the old pettifogging bastard had something he was a-skeered of. Had he did something to someone so bad that whoever he done it to might want to pay to get him killed for it? Now, the thing about that what really interested me was not so much that someone might be wanting to get rid of ole Peester or that Peester might be a-skeered of Sly so bad for personal reasons, but what really interested me was just what it mighta been that ole Peester had mighta did that was so bad. I wanted to know. I pulled my bottle and two glasses outa my desk drawer, early as it was, and I poured two drinks.

"Set down, Peester," I said, "and let's have us a drink and talk this here thing over."

"I don't need a drink," he said.

"You act to me like you do," I said.

"Barjack, it's way too early in the day," he said.

"Well, just set yourself," I said. "Pull up that chair over there."

He dragged the chair over and set right across my desk from me. I shoved the glass of whiskey over where he could reach it real easy, and I tuck my own self a drink.

"Mister Peester," I said, changing my previous harsh tone, "maybe I been a-dismissing your worries too casual. Maybe you had ought to tell me real calm-like just what it is about ole Sly a-being here that's got you so upset, and then maybe between the two of us, we can figger out a way to make him leave."

"Well, yes," he said. "Maybe so."

He reached over and picked up the glass I had put in front of him and tuck hisself a drink. He put the glass down again and harrumphed to clear his throat.

"Well," he said, "I know that Sly is a killer. He takes money to kill people he doesn't even know. He's cold-blooded. It seems to me that if he's spending time in our town, he must have a target here. Someone he's been paid to kill. It could be . . . anyone. You maybe."

"Or you?" I said.

He shuck his head real fast and nervous-like, making his loose lips and jaws flap. "No," he said. "No. Not me." He picked up the glass and tuck another swaller.

"Why not you?" I said. "Ain't there someone out there somewhere what might have it in for you bad enough to hire the ole Widdermaker? Hell, we all got our enemies, don't we?"

"There's no one with a reason to kill me," he said, but by damn, I coulda swore he was lying to me. I had never saw the little bastard so nervous. I'd saw him mad before, but not hand-shaking and jaw-flapping nervous like that.

"Who is it you're a-thinking mighta sent him here?" I said.

"No one," he said. "I tell you, it could be anyone. I—I've got to get back over to my office."

He got up fast and got his fat ass outa there, and I knowed then for sure that I had hit on a tender nerve with the ole mayor. He had did something bad to someone, and he was a-skeered that Sly had come to town just to get him. And whatever it was that he had did, he sure as hell didn't want me a-knowing nothing about it. Well, goddamn, I wanted to know. I wanted to know his honor's secret so damn bad, it was a-hurting me. I finished off my drink and what he had left of his, and I put the hat on my head and left out to go over to the Hooch House. Along the way, I seen Happy headed for the office.

"Happy," I said, "come on along with me."

"I was just going to the office," he said.

"I could see that," I said, "but I'm a-telling you to come along with me."

He turned and fell along beside me. "Where we going?" he asked me.

"Just come on along and don't ask so many damn questions," I said. I walked on to the Hooch House and inside, and Happy come along too. I ordered up a breakfast and some coffee. "You want anything?" I asked Happy.

"I done had my breakfast," he said. "I was going to work."

"You are at work," I said. "You want some coffee?"

"Sure," he said.

We got set down at a table with our coffee. I was still a-waiting for my breakfast to be brung out. I sipped a little coffee, and Happy did too, and then I said, "Happy, you was here in this town whenever I first come along, wasn't you?"

"Yeah," he said. "I reckon I was."

"How long was it you had been here?" I asked him.

"You mean whenever you first come to town?" he said.

"Ain't that what I just asked you?" I said. "I'll say it again real plain for a stupid head. Whenever I first come to town, how long was it you had done been here?"

"Ah, well," he said, "I don't rightly know. Maybe three or five years. I ain't sure, Barjack. Why you asking, anyhow? Is it important?"

"No," I said, "I'm just wasting time asking stupid questions."

"Oh," he said.

"Hell yes, it's important," I said. "Why else would I want to know?"

Sometimes I wished that I could come up with a bucket of brains somewhere and cut a hole in ole Happy's head and just pour them brains in there.

"I don't know," he said.

"All right," I said, "listen to me real careful now. I want you to tell me ever'thing you know about ole Peester—what he done and ever'thing—before I come to know him."

"Ever'thing?" Happy said.

"Ever'thing," I said.

"Well," said Happy, "whenever I first come to town,

87

he was already here, and he had his lawyering office over there where it's still at. Well, it ain't exactly the same office on accounta that time it got blowed up, and he went and had it rebuilt, but it was there in that same place. But only he weren't the mayor yet then. I don't mean whenever his office got blowed up. I mean whenever I first knowed him. He was just lawyering, that's all. He got hisself elected mayor just a year or so—no, maybe six months before you come along."

"All right," I said. "Go on."

"I don't know nothing more," he said.

Aubrey come out a-fetching my breakfast over to me just then, and whenever he set it down in front of me and started to turn around and go back toward the bar, I stopped him and made him set down, and I asked him the same questions I had just asked ole Happy. Aubrey, he leaned back and scratched his head.

"Well," he said, "Peester wasn't doing too well with his business. That's about all I recall. He was always in debt, you know, owing folks money he couldn't pay. Then whenever he got himself elected mayor and got a regular salary, things got a whole lot better for him."

"Whenever he was lawyering," I said, "was he persecuting or defending?" I asked that question, and then I picked up my fork and tied into that breakfast.

"I seem to recall that he done a little of both," Happy said. "Ain't that right, Aubrey?"

"I think he mostly defended when he was in court," Aubrey said. "Once he was prosecutor over at the county seat, but mainly he was suing folks. Like that time ole Singletree stumbled over the step out in front of Jonsey's store and hurt his knee, and ole Peester told Singletree that if he was to say he hurt his back, they could sue poor ole Jonsey and get a bunch of money out of him."

"Oh, yeah," said Happy. "I remember that now."

"Who's Jonsey?" I asked. "What store?"

"Well, Jonsey had the general store down there," Aubrey said, "till Peester sued him for ole Singletree. They got the store and everything away from Jonsey, and Jonsey up and left town."

"So where's this Singletree now?" I asked, 'cause I sure didn't know of no Singletree owning no store in Asininity.

"Oh, Singletree didn't want to own no store," Happy said. "He sold it out to Chester Filbert, and then he left town."

"So this here Singletree," I said, "and ole Peester made out like a couple of bandits on the deal. Right?"

"I reckon," Happy said.

"Peester acted as agent on the deal when Filbert bought the store, too," Aubrey said. "He come out a little more ahead then."

"All right," I said, between chewing on my breakfast, "let me see if I got all this straight. Peester was Singletree's lawyer, and he got paid for suing Jonsey, and then he got paid again for selling the store for Singletree. Right?"

"That's right," Aubrey said.

"That's how I recall it too," Happy said.

"And it was a crooked deal to begin with," I said. "Singletree's back never hurt him till Peester told him it should."

"I believe that's the way it happened," Aubrey said.

"So if anyone was to have it in for ole Peester over

that deal," I said, "it would be this here Jonsey?"

"Well, yeah," said Happy. "I reckon."

"So might Singletree," Aubrey said. "From what I heard, Peester wound up with more of the money on both deals than Singletree did."

Oh," I said. "I see. Does either one of you know of any other such deals our esteemed mayor had his sticky pettifogging fingers into?"

"There must have been," Aubrey said, "but just now I can't recall anything in particular."

"I can't think of nothing else," Happy said.

"Well, if either one of you comes up with anything else along them lines, let me know, you hear?" I said. "If that's all you can come up with right now, then that's all I need, except for some more coffee, Aubrey."

"Me too," said Happy.

"You don't need no more coffee," I said. "You get your ass on over to the office."

Happy pouted on outa the place, and Aubrey fetched the coffeepot over to pour me another cupful. "You seen ole Sly yet this morning?" I asked him.

"He came through a little while ago," Aubrey said. "I think he went across the street to get his breakfast."

"Oh, sure, he would," I said. "I shoulda knowed that without asking."

"Funny thing," Aubrey said.

"What?" I said. "Sly having breakfast at the White Owl?"

"No," said Aubrey. "I was still thinking about poor ole Singletree."

"What's funny, then?" I asked.

"Peester not only got all that money out of him," Aubrey said, "he also got Singletree's wife, at least for a while there."

"Set your ass back down here and tell me about it," I said.

"I don't really know too much about it," said Aubrey. "But I'll tell you who likely does know."

"Who's that?" I said.

"Miss Bonnie," he said. "She knew all about it. I think."

I swallered down the rest of my coffee and like to burnt my tongue off, and then I hurried up the stairs and went back to Bonnie's room. I had spent the night there, but whenever I had got up, she was still a-snoring away. Ole Bonnie always liked to sleep away half the morning. I went up there and barged right in through the door and moved on over to the bed and set down on it and slapped Bonnie on the ass. She yelped and jumped.

"What?" she said.

"Wake up, Bonnie," I said. "I got to talk to you."

She kinda half set up and went to rubbing her eyes with the back of her hand. God, she looked awful in the morning.

"Can't it wait?" she said.

"Hell no, it can't wait," I said. "If it could wait, I wouldn't be here."

"I can't wake up this early," she said. "What time is it, anyhow?"

"Hell, I don't know," I said. "Somewhere 'round seven, I guess."

"Seven!" she said, and she plopped herself back down and pulled the covers plumb up over her head. "Leave me alone."

"Bonnie," I said, slapping her ass again, "wake up, damn it."

"Get out of here, Barjack," she yelled.

It seemed hopeless, but I was determined, so I went back downstairs, and I seen that a few more folks had come into the place by then, but I weren't concerned none with that just then. I had more important things on my mind. I got the coffeepot and a cup from ole Aubrey and tuck them upstairs and poured Bonnie a cup of coffee.

"Here, sweet," I said. "I brung you some coffee in bed. Set up now and drink it. It'll help you wake up. I got something important to ask you about."

"Go away," she said.

I tuck hold of the covers and pulled them down from offa her face, and she turned over real quick-like and swung a right arm and smacked me right across the side of the head and knocked me clean offa the bed and sprawling onto the floor and the coffeepot and cup and all of that hot coffee went after me and like to scalded my chest and belly. I yowled out something fierce, and that made her set up all right.

"What's wrong?" she said.

"You like to burnt me to death," I said, "and that after you broke my goddamned jaw and wrenched my back, to boot."

"Did I do that?" she said. And she come outa that bed still stark staring nekkid, and she come a-flopping all that flesh at me and squatted down beside me. "I was asleep, honey," she said. "I didn't know what I was doing. Oh, sweetheart, are you hurt bad?"

"Look at me here," I said, and I pulled at my white

shirtfront there where it was all stained brown with coffee.

"Oh, baby," she said.

"And it's blistered my belly, too," I said. "And after I brung it to you in bed. When's the last time a man brung you your coffee in bed?"

"Here, sweetness," she said, "let me help you up."

She tuck hold of me and started in to pulling, and I groaned something fierce getting up to my feet. I twisted an arm around to kinda hold on to my back like as if I was about to die from the pain, and I limped over to a chair and set my ass down. She started into taking off my coat and vest and then went for my shirt, but I stopped her right there. I didn't have no intention of getting nekkid again. Well, then she went and reached under my shirt, and she glommed some kinda salve onto my poor ole blistered belly. She kept on a-saying sweet things and making over me all the time. Final, she led me back over to the bed, and we both laid down on it. She tuck my head and held it against her big left titty.

"Is it better, sweet'ums?" she said.

"I reckon I'll live," I said.

"What was it that was so urgent you had to come and try to wake me up so early in the morning and take your life in your hands like that?" she said.

"I need to know about ole Peester and the wife of a guy name of Singletree," I said. "Aubrey told me you'd know all about it."

Chapter Eight

By God, the next thing I knowed, I was flying headlong through the air. I had wondered a time or two, like I guess all men does now and then, just what it would be like to fly, and ole Bonnie, she sure showed me, and here's just the way she done it. She jumped up, dumping me flat on my back on the bed, and before I could even think about recovering some, she grabbed my shirtfront and pulled me up to where I was in a setting position. She hauled me forward just enough to clear the handles she wanted. Then she tuck me by the collars, all of them, from behind, and by the back side of my belt at the same time, and she lifted me right up to where I was a-swinging all fours in midair.

"Bonnie," I said, "put me down."

She run through that room and through the door and down the hall.

"What the hell're you doing, Bonnie?" I said.

I seen the stairway dead ahead, but the whole world was kinda swinging and swaying 'cause of my particular situation. "Bonnie," I said, "turn me loose," and she did, but it weren't just exactly what I had meant. What she done was she swung me back and forth three or four times in order to get herself a good powerful heave, and then she let go on a forward swing, and I went a-flying. I mean, she didn't just pitch me down the stairs. She flung me out and up, way over the stairs. I seen them stairs down there below me whilst I was a-flying.

I seen faces down there, too, a-looking up at me wild eyed and horrified, most likely thinking that they was a-fixing to see a death the like of which hadn't never been seen before on this earth, and they was more a them folks down there, too, than what was there whenever I had left a bit earlier. Some others had come in since then. I even seen ole Sly just step in through the front door, and I noticed that Happy had snuck his ass back in. I seen all that while I was up there a-flying.

Well, I was flying pretty good too, ole Bonnie had give me a hell of a start, so I tried to keep it up by flapping my wings and hoping that I might could at least give myself a softer landing or something, but it never worked. I had flew out at a slight angle, so whenever I final come down, I weren't right over the stairs no more. I was off to one side, and there was a table down below. There wasn't no one setting at it, and that was good, 'cause that was where I come down, and I come down hard. I landed flat on my belly, flat on top of that table. It cushioned my landing some. I'm convinced that it weren't near as hard as a floor landing woulda been. It tuck out all my air, though, and all I was thinking was that I had final quit flying, and I was still alive, and then all the legs give out together on that there table, and me and the tabletop tuck a hard drop to the floor. I believe that one hurt worser than the first landing. I also believe it was that last short drop to the floor that busted my nose.

I couldn't move. I couldn't breathe. I sure couldn't say nothing. I could hear, though, and I heard footsteps a-coming toward me. There was several of them, but they weren't in no hurry. It sounded kinda like whenever you've shot something and it's laying still but you ain't sure if you kilt it or not and so you're a-moving in real slow and easy. That's what it sounded like. But it was me they was moving in on. Then I made out ole Aubrey's voice.

"She fin'ly went and killed him," he said. "I always knew she would, sooner or later."

"You sure she kilt him?" said Happy, and I wished that I could talk so I coulda told him how stupid he was sounding just then.

"He ain't breathing," Aubrey said. "That usually means a man's dead, don't it?"

"It can mean a man's dead," said a calmer voice, and I could make it out to belong to ole Widdermaker hisself, and as he talked he come closer to me, "or it can mean that he's holding his breath for some reason, or his breath has all been knocked out of him."

Then I felt hands take aholt of me, and I heard Sly say, "Give me a hand here," and then I was rolled over onto my back, and I was staring straight up at Sly and ole Happy. They tuck holda my arms then and pulled me up to a setting position. They caught their own breath, then hauled me on up to my feet and commenced to walking, one on each side of me a-holding me up. By and by I started in to get some breath back. Soon as I felt like I had the strength back to support my own self, I waved my arms out, flinging the two of them offa me and standing alone, and then I kept on a-waving my arms some more after that, and each of my breaths was a little faster, deeper, and louder than the last one.

Well, it musta looked like as if I was a-going to try to fly again, but that weren't it at all. What I was doing was I was waving at Aubrey to come to me, and I was a-trying to get in enough breath to call out one time, and whenever I did get the breath enough, then I did yell out, and I said, "Whiskey." Then I just sorta fell backwards, and someone got a chair underneath my ass just in time, and I set down real heavy. Aubrey come a-running fast enough, and he handed me a tumbler full. I tuck it and started in to gulping. He stood there a-watching me, like as if he wanted to say something to me whenever I come up for air, but I guess he got tired of waiting. He reached back behind me and put the bottle down on the nearest table there. I come up for air. I set there breathing hard and heavy.

"Barjack," Aubrey said, "Your nose—"

"—is broke," I said. "Fix it for me." I tipped back the tumbler and gulped down the rest of the whiskey. Then I leaned my head back to give ole Aubrey a proper shot at me. You see, you don't need no doc to set no broke nose. Anyone can do it for you, if he's got the guts for it, and ole Aubrey, he had set my broke nose a time or two after some little brawls there in the Hooch House.

Aubrey, he kinda nodded at ole Happy, and Happy tuck a hard swaller and stepped up behind me. He got hisself a grip on my shoulders and I laid my head back into his gut, and Aubrey stepped on in. He put his left hand against the side of my head to hold it still, and then he felt around on my nose a little. Figgering it out, he placed a thumb against it and shoved hard, and I felt that ole nose slide across my face and kinda click back in place there where it was supposed to be at. I roared out, though, at the pain like a mama lion.

I set there holding my head in both my hands and a-blinking while the world kept a-changing from all red to all black with ever' blink of my eyeballs, and each blink was a throb too. I didn't hear no voices all during this time, so my sense of the situation is that ever'one in the place was just a-standing or setting around a-waiting to see how I was a-fixing to come outa all that. It come to me in the midst of all that silence that I had not picked a wise time to question ole Bonnie Boodle. Final, the red tuck over, and then it faded some. The pain from the snapping of my nose back into place begun to ease off. I set up straight. I looked around me to see where I was at. I seen my bottle on a table kinda behind me, so I turned my chair around to the table. Aubrey seen what I was a-doing, and he was right there. He picked up my tumbler from where I had dropped it on the floor, and he poured it full and set it in front of me.

"Are you all right, Barjack?" he asked me.

"I'm just fine," I said. "Hell, I'm wonderful. Any you men what ain't tried flying yet, by God, I recommend it right high. There ain't no sensation like it in the whole world. It's like you're a-soaring like a bird. Like a eagle.

Like you're riding on the wind. Why, you can look down and see all the folks down below all at one time, and you can see them looking up at you in very wonder at the magnificent fact of your flying over their heads."

Well, folks had caught on to me by then, and they seen that I wasn't dead, so they was beginning to chuckle a little, and so I added, "There's just only a couple of details I need to work on to make flying even better."

"What's that, Barjack?" Happy asked me.

"How to stay up there longer," I said, "and how to come down with a little more ease."

Why, then they bursted out laughing at me, and ole Aubrey, he was selling the beer and whiskey in kinda record volume for that time of the day. So I figgered that the whole entire morning weren't going to turn out to be a total loss and a waste after all. Then I tried to recall just what it was that I had wanted to know about so bad, but I couldn't pull the thought up outa my brain, what was some addled just then, as I'm sure you'll understand why.

"Set down, Happy," I said, and he set across from me. I looked around, and I seen ole Sly still a-standing. I give him a wave, and he come a-walking over. "Set a spell with us," I said. "I reckon you've done et, but I'll stand you for some more coffee—or whatever else you might be in mind of drinking this fine morning."

Sly tuck a seat to Happy's right. He give me a smile. "I believe I'll have a drink of your fine whiskey with you, Marshal," he said, "in honor of your first day of flight. You achieved what Icarus achieved but failed to live to tell about. You, on the other hand, have given us a marvelous description of the sensation of flight."

During all that, Aubrey had stuck a glass down in front of Sly, and he poured it full. Sly lifted it up like as if for a toast. "To Icarus and Barjack," he said. "Two expressions of the highest nobility of the human spirit."

Well, now, what with my recent somewhat earth-shattering experience, all of them big words ole Sly was a-spewing begin to work on my head and cause it to spin some more. I weren't at all sure but what I was being set up and poked fun at, and I sure didn't care for that none, no matter what if it was the Widdermaker a-doing the funning.

"What was that other feller's name?" I said.

"Icarus?" Sly said.

"Yeah," I said. "That's the one. Ickrus. Tell me about that there Ickrus. Just what did he do?"

"Icarus was a Greek," said Sly. "The son of a fisherman, but he wanted more out of life. He had great aspirations. He wanted to fly, Barjack, just as you. He collected a great many feathers from the largest birds around, and when he had enough, he built himself a pair of wings, using wax to stick the feathers together and then to attach the completed wings to his own back and arms. Then he went to the highest hill, and he jumped off. He flapped his wings, and he could indeed fly. You see, Barjack, he mastered the first of the two problems you yourself mentioned—the problem of how to stay up longer. The wings solved that problem for him . . . almost."

"Almost?" I said. "What happened?"

"He flew too high and stayed too long in the hot sun,"

Sly said. "The wax melted, and poor Icarus plunged to his death."

"Aw, the poor bastard," I said. "Well, I ain't going to have that problem nohow, 'cause I ain't going to stick no feathers all over myself with no wax. I done been flying without no feathers."

"And you came down," said Sly, "and lived to tell about it. You're already way out ahead of Icarus. You are the current champion of free, unassisted flight."

"Well, now, Mister Sly," I said, "that sounds good, but I ain't so sure about it. That there Ickrus, he musta got hisself up there real high in order for the sun to melt that there wax and all. How high do you s'pose he got?"

"The actual height was never recorded," Sly said. "I suppose if we had been there to watch, Icarus would have appeared to us as a high-flying eagle or hawk in the sky."

"That high, huh?" I said. "Well, now, you see, I ain't never even come close to that. I weren't even outside, and so I had this here roof in my way. Besides, I got to work on my slowing-down and landing techniques before I take my ass up that high."

"I can understand that," Sly said.

Right then ole Sly was a-keeping up with me drink for drink, and ever'one else in the place seemed to be just content in a-watching and a-listening to the two of us whilst we went on and on embellishing the tale of my flight and adding to the old story about Ickrus and how whenever he tried the same thing, he got hisself killed. By and by, though, as new ones come in, why, they didn't know what the hell we was talking about, so someone would have to tell them the whole thing from the beginning. Once I overheard someone, I don't know who, saying, "And then I looked up, and I seen ole Barjack just a circling this very room, right up there over my head."

It sounded to me like as if someone had started a fight over by the front door, but I was feeling too good to let it worry me. Happy come over, though, and he said, "Barjack, a couple of cowhands is trying to bust the place up over there."

"Handle them, Happy," I said.

"Yes, sir," he said. He tuck on off through the crowd, and then I decided I wanted to watch ole Happy do his job. I leaned over so I could see better. That didn't work. I had to stand up.

"What is it, Barjack?" Sly said.

"Stand up here a minute and let's watch ole Happy take on them drunk cowboys over yonder," I said.

"Oh," said Sly, and he kinda lurched up to his feet. He was a-looking around the room, which had done got good and crowded by this time, and I pointed Sly in the right direction. Ole Happy had learnt good, I can tell you that. He didn't call out no warnings nor nothing. He walked right up behind the first of them two fighting cowboys, pulled out his Colt, and banged it down hard on the man's head. As the man crumpled on down to the floor, clearing the air between his opponent and ole Happy, the one left standing, the opponent, suddenly was a-looking in the barrel of Happy's Colt 'stead of at the fists of the other cowboy. Happy cocked the Colt, and the cowboy stood still.

"Unbuckle your gunbelt and drop it on the floor," Happy said, and the cowboy done it. "Now get his and put it over there with yours," said Happy. The cowboy done that. Then Happy said, "All right, grab aholt on your buddy somewheres, 'cause you're a-taking him along with yourself on over to the jailhouse."

I watched just a little more after that, just till the cowboy had commenced dragging the deadweight of his former sparring partner toward the door, and then I set my ass back down. I was some wobbly on my feet anyhow. So was Sly. He damn near missed the chair whenever he set back down, but he never. He made it all right. "Happy done that just right," I said. "Just the way I taught him to do it. I ain't going to tell him that, though. Can't have him getting cocky on me, you know."

"Heaven forbid," Sly slurred.

Of a sudden, ole Bonnie plopped her fat ass down right next to me, and leaned over close at me, and give me a simpering look. I hadn't even knowed that she had come down the stairs. Sly tipped his hat. "Baby," she said to me, "you're all right, ain't you?"

"No thanks to you," I said. "You committed attempted murder on my person. You damn near killed me, and you did break my nose. The last fella what went through what you just put me through, fella name of Ickrus, was kilt outright."

"Oh, baby," she said, "don't be mad at me. You know how I am in the mornings."

"Next time you take a notion in your head to kill me," I said, "just tell me. I'll make it easy on you." I pulled out my Merwin and Hulbert Company revolver, cocked it, and laid it on the table with the barrel aimed right smack dab at my own chest. The butt was within easy grasp for Bonnie. It got real quiet around us. Folks heard that click, and they seen me lay down that gun like I done it. "You want to kill me," I said, "there's the gun. It's loaded, and it's cocked. Hell, it's even aimed for you. All you got to do is just pull the trigger. That's all."

"I don't want to kill you, Barjack," she said.

"You don't?" I said. "Why, it'd sure be damned hard as hell to convince anyone who was in here for my Ickrus act of the fact of what you just said."

"Huh?" she said.

"I mean," I said, "that anyone who seen my high-flying act this morning would sure as hell thought that you meant to kill me dead. That's what I meant."

She looked over at Sly, and he kinda shrugged. She looked back at me, and then she done the one thing I was hoping she wouldn't do, but I shoulda knowed she would do it. Ever' time it looked like as if I was about to get the best of her in a situation like that there, she done it. She done it as a last way of finishing me off and winning the fight or the argument or just coming out on top of the situation. She went to crying.

It started with just her lips a-quivering, and a little pout on her face. She brung up a tear from somewhere, and it commenced real slow-like to running out the corner of her eye. Her cheeks was so fat, it just set there on top of her cheek for spell with no place to run to. Then she started in to talk, and her voice was little and quivery.

"I didn't know what I was doing, baby," she said. "I wouldn't hurt you on purpose. Not for the whole world, I wouldn't. You know that. I love you, honey."

"Aw, Bonnie," I said, "hell, don't go to bawling now."

"But I didn't mean to do you no harm," she blubbered. I reached around her as far as I could and give her a squeeze.

"Hell," I said, "it's all right. Why, it give us the best story what the Hooch House has ever had anyhow. Folks'll be telling that one over and over from now on, and it'll be told from here to Denver."

"Why, the tale of your Icarian flight will be set to ballad lines," said Sly. "To Denver? Why, the words will fly through Denver to Seattle, Portland, Sacramento, San Francisco, Los Angeles, and thence across the ocean to China."

Bonnie give me a look at that. "Is Mister Sly . . . drunk?" she said.

"You're a-looking at him," I said.

"St. Louis," Sly said, "Kansas City, Omaha, Chicago, New York, London, Paris."

"It did make a hell of a story," I said. Just then ole Sly stood up straight, but when he done that, he knocked into the table, and my Merwin and Hulbert Company revolver went a-sliding off and hit the floor, and being cocked the way I left it, why, it just natural discharged. Bonnie screamed, and Sly fell over backwards. Guns come out all over the room, with their owners a-looking for something to shoot back at, but of course, there wasn't nothing. To emphasize that plain and simple fact, drunk as I was, I reached down for that fallen revolver and picked it up by the barrel and held it up high so ever'one could see me.

"Ever'thing's all right," I hollered. I tucked the Merwin and Hulbert back into the holster, where it belonged in the first place. "Just a little accident over here is all."

The guns was put away then, and there was even some chuckling around the room. Sly come a-crawling up from offa the floor where he had fell to. He stood up and straightened hisself as best he could. Then, still trying to be dignified, he said, "I believe it's early enough in the day that I can still sleep this one off in time. I'm going to my room."

He touched the brim of his hat in that there grand gentleman gesture of his, turned, and staggered on toward the stairs. I watched him make it about halfway to the top, and then I quit watching. I pulled ole Bonnie on over closer to me.

"Do you for real not want to kill me no more?" I asked her.

"Barjack," she protested. "I never did."

"All right, sweet," I said. "All right. I believe you. Let's you and me take our bottles and glasses and go on back upstairs, then. What do you say to that little idee?"

She wriggled herself all against me and slobbered on the side of my head.

"That's a wonderful idea," she said. "Let's go."

"Only thing is," I said, as I sort of lurched upright, "you got to kinda keep me on my feet till we get our asses up there."

"I can do that for my sweet cakes," she said.

"And then once we get there—"

We staggered on a few steps together.

"What?" she said. "What else?"

"You got to watch out for my poor ole nose what you broke only just this morning," I said. "You can't go bumping into it nor nothing like that, 'cause it's still awful tender to the touch."

"I'll be real careful of your tender nose, sweet cakes," Bonnie said, "but you got some other tender places that I mean to attack real hard."

106

Chapter Nine

I don't know what the hell time it was. We had slept some, and we had fooled around some, kinda back and forth, you know, and when I was awake, I drunk me some more whiskey. It was dark night, though, so I reckon we had been at it most of the day. That's the best I can do about the time. Someone commenced to banging on the door and a-calling my name. Ole Bonnie set up faster than what I did, and she hollered out, "Who's that?"

"It's Aubrey, Miss Bonnie," come the answer. "I need Barjack."

"What the hell do you need in the middle of the goddamn night?" I said.

"There's a mob, Barjack," Aubrey said. "They're fixing to hang Mister Sly."

I got my nekkid ass up outa the bed and banged the

big toe of my left foot against something there in the dark. I was hopping around on one foot and a-cussing. "Damn it, Bonnie," I said, "get a damn light on." She found a match and struck it and lit the lamp on the table.

"Go'get Happy," I yelled.

"They done knocked Happy out," Aubrey said. "He's laying in the floor downstairs."

"Damn it," I said. I was pulling on my britches, and Bonnie throwed a robe on and tied it around her waist. She brung me my boots, and I pulled them on. Then I pulled on my shirt and grabbed my gunbelt and strapped it on. I headed out the door half-dressed like that. I damn near run into ole Aubrey when I went out the door. "Come on, Aubrey," I said.

"Barjack," said Bonnie. "Be careful."

"What do you want with me?" Aubrey said, kinda whining.

I was already headed down the stairs. "Just come on," I said, and he did. We got down into the main room of the Hooch House, and I told him, "Get that shotgun out from behind the bar and come with me."

"I ain't no deputy," he said.

"You are if I say so," I told him. "Get the shotgun or I'll shoot you dead right now."

While he was a-getting the shotgun, I seen right where ole Happy was laid out, and I went over to check on him. He was out cold all right, and there was blood caked on the back of his head. Someone had belted him a good one across his noggin. I was glad he had such a thick skull, but I could see right off that he weren't going to be no help. "Come on, Aubrey," I said. "Where'd they go?"

I started on out the door, and Aubrey come after me a-toting that scattergun. He weren't none too happy about it, though.

"They clobbered Happy," he said, "and they grabbed ole Sly from behind. I guess they knowed that he was too drunk to really defend himself, and they figured you was out for the night too. They dragged Sly out the front door and headed north down the street."

I headed north, and Aubrey come right along with me. I reckon he was more skeered of me than he was of that mob.

"How many of them?" I said.

"I don't know," he said. "A dozen at least."

I figgered I knowed where they went, all right. There was a big old elum tree just outside of town on the north end. If they was a hanging mob, that's where they'd be going. Me and Aubrey hurried along on foot, 'cause I figgered that we could get there faster thataway than taking time to saddle up a couple of horses. I was huffing and puffing by the time we got to where we could see some fire up ahead and could hear some angry voices. "Come on," I said.

They was up there, all right, and they was so intent on their dirty business and making so much noise that they never knowed we was coming up on them. The fire we had saw was coming from torches that some of them was carrying to light their wicked way. They had ole Sly mounted up on a ole gray horse with his hands tied behind his back. I seen Marty Bodene on a horse, too. He rode up under the old elum and tossed a rope up over a big branch. He already had a hanging noose tied in one end.

Whenever that noose come down, ole Marty tuck the other end of the rope and wrapped it around the trunk of the tree several times. Then he rode up beside poor ole Sly, and he was fixing to fit that noose over Sly's head. Me and Aubrey was pretty close by then. I hauled out my Merwin and Hulbert Company revolver and fired off a shot into the night sky. Ever'one shut up and turned. "All right, goddamn it," I yelled, "ever'one of you bastards turn around and go home right now before I get mad."

"You can't stop us, Barjack," ole Marty said. "They's too many of us for you."

"I can kill you dead with one shot, Marty," I said, "and by God, I will too, if you don't drop that noose right now."

"You do that, Barjack," Marty said, "and you'll go straight to hell with me. Ten men will put bullets in you."

"Not if ole Aubrey here cuts loose with his scattergun first," I said. "Aubrey, whenever I kill ole Marty, you pull your triggers. You hear me? You don't even need to aim at no one. Just point that greener general into the crowd."

Aubrey never said nothing, and that was likely for the best, 'cause if he had tried to talk, they'd have heard how skeered he was in his quivering voice.

"Don't let him bluff you, boys," Marty said. "Hell, we're all citizens here. Barjack knows us. He ain't going to kill us to save no professional killing man."

"What you're fixing to do here is a murder," I said, "and I'll damn sure kill you to keep you from doing a murder. Now, you drop that damn noose like I told you to do."

Ole Marty was part right. He knowed he had me at least in a standoff. As long as he weren't making no move toward Sly, I weren't about to just shoot him off his horse for setting there holding a rope. And I didn't have no way of knowing what ole Aubrey would do if it really come to shooting. Likely, he'd just toss that shotgun to one side, fall down flat and cover up his head, and wait for the shooting to stop. If it was to come to that, I figgered I'd be deader'n hell in just a few minutes. I had to bluff them out. That's all there was to it. I started walking toward ole Marty.

"Stay back, Barjack," he said.

"You going to go for your gun, Marty?" I asked him. " 'Cause I already got you covered. I'll kill you before you get the damn thing out, and you'll be dead before you hit the ground."

"Spread out, boys," Marty said.

Now, that was the smartest thing he coulda said, and some of the rest of that mob started in to doing just that. I stopped moving in on him then, 'cause if I was to move in any closer, I wouldn't be able to keep a eye on them that was spreading to both sides. I shifted my eyeballs' from one side to the other, watching to see if anyone was pulling a gun.

"Keep moving, boys," Marty said. "We'll have them surrounded in a minute."

"Stand still, damn it," I said.

"Who's in control here now, Barjack?" Marty said.

"I know ever' one of you bastards," I said. "Are you planning on killing me here tonight too? 'Cause you better be if you go on with this. If you do this thing tonight and leave me alive, I'll get ever' damn one of you later. I mean that."

"We'll worry about that later," Marty said.

By then I had lost sight of the men farthest out on the flanks. They had me surrounded, and that's for sure. Well, I tell you, I didn't know what the hell to do then. I could go on ahead and kill ole Marty, for all the good it woulda did. Them others woulda just gone on ahead and shot me down from all sides, and ole Aubrey, hell, he wouldn't do nothing, like I said before. Then with me dead, they'd go on ahead and hang ole Sly, and I'd be dead for nothing. This thing weren't working out at all the way I had meant for it to. I had thought that I'd just buffalo all of them ole boys and that would be that, but it didn't turn out like that at all.

Just then two men come up behind me and one of them grabbed me on each side by a arm. I fired a shot, but it went harmless into the ground, and then someone come up and wrenched my Merwin and Hulbert outa my hand. I was twisting and jerking and kicking and cussing till a third one come up behind me and reached a arm around my throat and commenced to choking me. I was too busy fighting to know what ole Aubrey was a-doing, but the one thing I did know was that he never fired off no shotgun. I shoulda knowed not to trust Aubrey to back me up.

"Just hold on to him, boys," Marty said, "till we get this one here strung up."

I roared and growled, and I could feel my face puffing up and turning red. I knowed I couldn't fight them much longer. And busy as I was, I could see that son of a bitch

Marty slip that noose down around ole Sly's neck. I can tell you right now for sure and certain, I been in some bad scrapes, but I don't recollect ever being so damn skeered in my whole life. I weren't skeered that they would really kill me, although I guess that there was a distinct and real possibility, but what I was really a-skeered of was that they was going to hang ole Sly right then and there and right in front of me with me helpless as a babe.

Well, somehow I managed to slip my chin down under the arm what was choking my neck, and I got my mouth open wide and tuck me a hell of a bite outa that fella's arm. He screamed like hell and turned loose of me, and I guess that startled them others just enough that I was able to make a move on them then, and I swung both of my arms forward in such a way that I knocked them two bastards together. That jarred them loose from my arms, and then I grabbed their two heads and bashed them together real good and proper.

I went running for Aubrey's shotgun then, 'cause there weren't no way I could find my own Merwin and Hulbert in time to do no good. I jerked the gun outa Aubrey's hands, but someone whacked me across of the back of my head, and I went down to my knees a-seeing stars. I weren't out, though, and I seen Marty give that ole gray horse a slap on the ass, and it run forward and right out from under Sly. Sly went to swinging. Then I heard a rifle shot from my right, and I seen ole Marty fall outa his saddle. A shotgun went off somewhere off to my left, and a rider come into the middle of things lickety-split and rode right up to ole Sly and grabbed on to him.

"The next one to move is a dead son of a bitch," I heard someone say. And I'll be goddamned if it weren't ole Bonnie's voice. I tried to shake my head clear, and then I seen that Sly was setting on a horse with Lillian, and she was a-loosening that damn noose so she could slip it offa his head. I got up to my feet and kinda staggered over to where ole Marty was a-lying. I nudged at him with my toe. He was dead. The next voice I heard belonged to ole Happy Bonapart hisself.

"All of you drop your guns right now," he said. "Any wrong moves and you're dead."

Well, all the mobsters shucked their irons, all right. Hell, they didn't know how many they was up against nor where all they was at out there in the dark. Whenever they was all stripped of their weapons, Happy made them move in and bunch up together. Then he come in and stood there beside me, and Bonnie come in from the other side. She was a-carrying a Marlin. It had been Bonnie what had kilt ole Marty. Goddamn, I was proud of her.

"What now, Marshal?" Happy said.

"You done a pretty damn good job up till now," I said. "What do you say?"

"Well," Happy said, "I guess I'd say take them all in and lock them up."

"Let's do that, Depitty," I said.

Happy and Bonnie started in to marching the mob, minus ole Marty of course, toward the jailhouse, and I walked over to where Lillian and Sly was still a-setting on her horse. I looked up at ole Sly.

"You all right?" I asked him.

"I think so," he said. "Thanks to all of you."

"Lillian," I said, "you'd oughter take him to see ole Doc anyhow, just to be sure."

"I will," she said.

They rid on off, and I nosed around till I found my Merwin and Hulbert. Then I turned to foller Happy and Bonnie a marching the mob off to jail. I caught up with Bonnie and walked along beside her. "You all sure come in the nick of time," I said.

"We come as fast as ever we could, sweetness," Bonnie said. "Fast as you went out the door, I got a wet rag and mopped ole Happy's face till he come to. I told him what happened, and we headed out after you when we seen Lillian come outa the White Owl closing up for the night. I told her what was going on, and she grabbed that horse that was there at a hitching rail. Don't know who owns it. Anyhow, when we got close enough to see what was happening, me and Happy started in to shooting, and Lillian rode in fast to save Mister Sly from hanging."

"All three of you done good," I said.

"You done all right yourself, Barjack," she said.

"Hell," I said, "they had me whipped."

"You didn't have no help," she said, "and you held them off all by your lonesome long enough for us to get there."

Well, by God, I guessed she was right at that. I felt pretty good then. I felt good about my own self and about my depitty and about my sweet thing and even about my nagging bitch of a wife. I guessed I knowed who I could trust in a pinch. Ole Aubrey was dragging his chicken ass along behind us real slow and dejected-like. He had picked up that shotgun again after I had let it drop when the danger was over. I slowed down a little and waited for him. I tuck the gun away from him.

"Go on back to the Hooch House, Aubrey," I said. "Hell, someone might be in there a-drinking up all my whiskey without paying for it."

He turned toward the Hooch House, and I kept on a-follering the others to the jailhouse. I thought about chewing Aubrey's ass out, but then I decided that it wouldn't do no good to tell a chicken what a chicken he was, so I just let it go. He was a good bartender. When I got to the jailhouse right behind ole Bonnie, Happy already had the whole entire hanging mob in the two jail cells what we had and had locked the doors on them. Locked in like that, they got bold again, and they commenced to hollering.

"You can't lock us up like this. We're citizens."

"Let me outa here."

"I got a family to go home to."

I just pointed that shotgun at the ceiling over the cells and pulled the trigger. The roar inside the jailhouse was hellacious, and them shotgun pellets went to bouncing all over the place. Them bold hangmen went to hopping and dancing and yelping around, bumping into each other and falling over. I let that go on for a spell, then I said, "You want another one?" They shut up.

I walked over close to the cell still a-holding that shotgun. "You sons of bitches," I said, "came damn near to killing a man tonight. Your goddamned shenanigans did get one man killed. I aim to charge each one of you with attempted murder, assaulting a officer the law, conspiracy to commit a killing, being the cause of the killing of ole Marty, and any other damn thing I can think up.

So don't go talking about who and what you are, 'cause you ain't nothing to me but a bunch a criminals now, and you sure ain't going to get no special treatment in my jail. Shut up now and keep quiet."

Well, they did. I turned around and found ole Bonnie, and I went over to her and put a arm around her shoulders. She was still a-toting that Marlin. "Sweet," I said, "let's you and me get on back over to the Hooch House."

"I'll stay here and keep a eye on this bunch," Happy said.

I thought about that a second or two. Happy had been knocked silly earlier in the evening, and then he had come out of it and come on out to my rescue. I didn't feel like watching no jail full of bastards, and I was sure that he didn't neither.

"Naw, Happy," I said, "you come on along with us. Hell, they're locked up good. They don't need no watching."

"You sure, Barjack?" Happy said.

"Come on," I said.

The three of us went on outside, and I seen Lillian and Sly coming outa the doc's office. We met them in the middle of the street.

"Well," I said, "what'd Doc say?"

"He says I'm in real good shape for a man that just got himself hanged," Sly said.

Lillian was holding on to his left arm like she thought he might get away from her. It didn't seem to bother her none that I was right there.

"Well," I said, "that whole bunch is locked up. They won't be causing no more trouble."

"I want to thank you, Marshal," Sly said. "All of you."

"Hell," I said, "me and Happy, we was just doing our jobs. The ladies here, well, they're something special now. Both of them."

"I still thank all of you," said Sly. "If there's anything I can do for you—"

"There is one little thing," I said.

"Name it," said Sly.

"How would you like to be a depitty for a little while?" I said.

Well, now, let me tell you, you shoulda saw the faces on that bunch of prisoners whenever I walked back into the jailhouse with ole Sly, and I told them that I had just appointed him a special depitty, and he was a-going to be watching over things for the night. Their eyes all got as big as saucers, and then ole Sly, he pulled out his both six-guns, and he commenced to twirling them on his trigger fingers, and tossing them in the air and catching them, and tossing them from one hand to the other. I never seen such carrying on with a couple of six-guns as what he was a-doing. I guess that bunch thought that whenever I left outa there, ole Sly just might commence to shooting off their ears one at a time or something. I never did see such a skeered bunch. It done my heart good to leave them like that with Sly a-standing guard. I headed on to the Hooch House to join Bonnie and Happy. Sly and me had done walked Lillian home before we went back on over to the jail. When I went into the Hooch House and found Bonnie and Happy a-setting together in there, ole Happy, he said, "Where you been, Barjack?"

"Well, Happy," I said, "I got to thinking about what you said, and I figgered you was right. That many prisoners in the jail, there really had ought to be a guard on duty. So I hired us a new guard for the night."

"Oh, yeah?" he said. "Who'd you hire?"

"Why, I hired the only man in town besides you that I can trust, ole pardner," I said. "I hired on ole Sly."

Happy and Bonnie both looked at me for a few seconds with kinda blank expressions on their faces, and then it come to them both at about the same time, and they burst out a-laughing.

Chapter Ten

Well, I had to keep that bunch of assholes in my damn jailhouse for two whole entire nights before the stage come into town with a scheduled run for the county seat and no passengers in it. I bought up all the space and paid for it with town money and crammed them bastards into the coach. Then, whenever it was time for the stage to roll on out, I clumb up on top with the driver, ole Goose Neck, and Ash Face, the shotgun guard, and we all rid on over to the county seat. I turned them prisoners over to Dick Custer, the county sheriff there, and made my charges, and he promised to let me know whenever they was scheduled for trail. I'd have to go back over there for that, and I'd likely have to take along ole Happy and ole Sly both as witnesses. I decided to spend the night there and go on back to Asininity the next day.

I got good and drunk that night and bought myself a

whore and had a whale of a good time and charged it all to the town of Asininity. After all, I was over at the county seat on town business. Then it turned out I had to wait another day before the stage would make another run back to my town, so I played around some more on town money. When I final got my ass back home, everything was real quiet. The stage rolled into town in the late afternoon. I got off and went right straight on into the Hooch House and found Happy and Bonnie setting there together. They acted right tickled to see me back as I set down with them, and ole Aubrey brung me a tumbler of my favorite whiskey.

"Where's ole Sly?" I asked them.

Happy kinda ducked his head, but ole Bonnie piped right up, "He's likely over at the White Owl. He's been spending a lot of his time over there the last couple of days. Ever' night, he walks Lillian home. From what I can tell, he ain't gone into the house with her yet, though."

"Hell," I said, "I don't give a damn if he does. Me and Lillian is quits. You know that, Bonnie. What she does and who she does it with is her business."

"It don't bother you none?" she said.

"Not a damn bit," I said.

She glommed onto my arm and snuggled up to me then, and she had a big grin on her face. "I'm glad to hear it, Barjack," she said. "You're all mine again."

"Ever' damn bit of me," I said.

Just about then ole Peester come in, and his face was red, and he was a-puffing. He stalked right over to where I was a-setting, and he said, "Barjack, I need to talk to you."

"Talk away, Mister Mayor," I said.

"It's business," he said. "You might want to make it more private."

"I don't need no secrets from Happy and Bonnie here," I said. "Go on ahead and say whatever it is you want to say. Set down and have a drink."

"No, thank you," Peester said. He stood there a-glaring at me for a few more seconds before he could bring hisself to say anything serious. Then, "Well, you finally did it, didn't you?" he said.

"What're you talking about, Peester?" I said.

"You finally got someone arrested," he said, "but you got the wrong people. You got some of our best citizens locked up over in the county jail on serious charges, and that professional killer is still free and walking our streets."

"Peester," I said, "you better go on back to pettifogging school and take a refresher course. We been all over this before. Herman Sly ain't broke no laws here. There ain't no reason to run him outa town nor to arrest him. That bunch I tuck over to the county jail was attempting to kill him, and I charged them all with attempted killing, and that's what they're fixing to get tried for. What's more, one of them got killed in the process, and according to what I was told over at the county seat, they're most likely going to be charged with aiding and abetting that killing—or something like that. And they attacked a officer of the law—me. Now, you take your fat ass on home and mind your business and let me mind the marshaling business before I get to asking you some questions about ole Singletree."

"What? Why—"

He went to blustering around like that for a bit, and he spit all over the front of his vest. Final, he got his tongue again, and he said, "What do you know about Singletree?"

"I know enough," I said, but of course, that was a lie. The way things had worked out, I never had got a chance to set down with ole Bonnie and get her to tell me the whole story. But I knowed from the way ole Peester was a-taking it that I was onto something all right. "Just go on home and settle your ass down," I said.

He turned around and hurried on outa there. Then I said, "Bonnie, I reckon now's a good time for it. Tell me about Peester and Singletree."

"Oh, well," she said, "ole Peester got a bunch of money out of poor ole Jonsey for Singletree. Got Jonsey's store too, and then sold it. Jonsey left town, and so did Singletree, but I think that Peester wound up with most of the money."

"I done heard all that," I said. "But I also heard there was something to do with ole Singletree's wife."

"Well, yeah, in a way," she said.

"What do you mean, in a way?" I said. "What happened?"

"Well, best I can recall," she said, "while Peester still had ever'thing in court, he got to spending some time with Agnes. That was Singletree's wife, Agnes. But then something happened that embarrassed all of them, and there's a couple of different stories about it. I ain't for sure which one is the right one."

"Tell me all of them," I said.

"The first one was that Peester couldn't get it up," Bonnie said. "Him and Agnes was both embarrassed over that, and Singletree was embarrassed that Peester was knowed to be messing with his wife, and that even a man who couldn't get it up had took his wife away from him. Right after that, Peester won the case, got the money and the store, and the Singletrees left town. Peester was supposed to sell the store and send the money on to them, but if he ever sent any money, it wasn't near what he got for the store."

"Well, that's a pretty good one, all right," I said. "What's the other'n?"

"The other story's total different," Bonnie said. "The way the other story went, it weren't Peester and Agnes at all what was messing around."

"Oh?" I said. "Who, then?"

Bonnie looked around to make sure no one else was a-listening to her, and even then she leaned in real close to me so that I could smell her hot breath whenever she talked. "It were Peester and Singletree," she said.

"What?" I said.

"It were Peester and Singletree," she said.

"You mean, ole Peester and this here Singletree was a-doing it together—in bed?" I said.

"That's the story," she said. "And whenever Agnes found out about them, she threatened to tell the whole town if Singletree didn't cut it off."

"You mean the stuff what was going on with Peester," I said. "You don't mean his thing?"

"No," Bonnie said, like as if she was kinda disgusted with me. "I mean that Agnes told Singletree if he didn't stop messing around with ole Peester, she was a-going to tell on them, and she was a-going to tell it ever'where, too. Well, he musta agreed to her terms, 'cause they left town right after that."

"And you don't know which story is the true story?" I asked her.

"No," she said. "I don't, but them was the two stories what got told all around town. After Singletree and Agnes left, folks eventual kinda forgot about it all after a while."

I scratched my head. I rubbed my chin. I drunk all of the whiskey outa my tumbler and then poured me some more.

"So," I said, "if ole Peester is a-skeered that Sly mighta come to town to kill him, and if the first tale is the true one, Peester might be a-thinking that ole Singletree hired Sly on account of him stealing his money and his wife."

"That could be," said Bonnie.

"It'd make sense," Happy agreed.

"But if the second story is the real one," I said, "then Peester could be a-thinking that it was Agnes what hired Sly. Either way, it could very easy be the whole damn Singletree incident what has got him running so skeered."

"From what all I know," said Bonnie, "that's what I'd say."

"Yeah," said Happy. "Me too."

"There's another possibility in all this what just come to me," I said. "That Jonsey feller could be a-trying to get even for what Peester done to him."

"Yeah," said Happy. "That's right, Barjack."

"I hadn't thought of that," said Bonnie, "but it could be."

"What I mean," I said, "is that them is all the different things what Peester could be a-thinking. We know ain't none of them true, 'cause we know that Sly never really come here to kill no one."

Well, I let all that soak into my head real good while I sipped me some more good whiskey. It come to me then that our troubles over ole Sly being in town was just about all behind us now. Now that I knowed all about the Singletree business, I could keep ole Peester shut up. There wasn't no question about that. The ranchers' feud was over, and now all the serious troublemakers was in jail over to the county seat. I figgered that things was going to get real quiet again and stay thataway, and that was the way I liked it. Sly come walking in just then. I waved at him, calling him on over to our table. He come on and set down with us.

"You want some whiskey?" I asked him.

"I think I'd best leave it alone," he said. "That last episode taught me a lesson. I seldom drink like that. I guess I had gotten a little too relaxed around here."

"Hell," I said, "that's all over and did with. There ain't no danger here now. Let me buy you a drink."

"I suppose one drink won't hurt anything," he said.

I called out to ole Aubrey to bring Sly a drink, and he did, but I noticed that ole Sly just kinda sipped at it, taking it real easy and staying cautious like. Thinking about how he damn near got hisself hanged, I guessed that I couldn't really blame him none too much for a-taking that there attitude. Anyhow, I was feeling pretty damn good, and I figgered we had plenty of cause for celebrating, and I meant to get my own self good and damn drunk.

I was a-thinking about ole Sly and my Lillian and the way they was a-getting so tight and how folks was a-talking about them all over town. It kinda tickled me how Sly was being such a gentleman, a-walking her home in the evening and not going inside the house and all, and me knowing Lillian the way I done, I figgered that his gentlemanliness was just driving her up the damn walls. I knowed that she was inviting him in ever' night, and he was too much of a gentleman to accept her invite. I knowed that was making her crazy too, and that was what was tickling me so much about it all. I was a-getting me a lotta satisfaction over Lillian being frustrated thataway. Far as I was concerned, she deserved it.

Well, by and by ole Happy opined as how he'd had enough and needed to get hisself some sleep before it was time for him to be at the office in the morning, and I never tried to stop him, 'cause I sure didn't want to have to be there too damn early. He went on then, and that left just only me and Bonnie and Sly. Bonnie excused herself and went over to the bar to tell one of the girls something, and so while it was just me and Sly a-setting there, he decided to talk at me about something.

"Barjack," he said, "you know that there's no one who can make me leave a town if I don't want to go."

"Yeah," I said, "I reckon I kinda had that one all figgered out."

"But if you want me to leave your town," he said, "just give me the word, and I'll leave."

I wrinkled my face up some, 'cause I sure as hell didn't know what the hell he was a-talking about. "Why the hell would I want you to go?" I asked him. "Hell,

I'm the one what's been defending your right to be here."

"I know that," he said. "You've been upholding the law. But it should be pretty obvious to you by now, as well as to everyone else in town, that I have an interest in Mrs. Barjack. More than a passing interest. You say the word, and I'll leave."

"Mr. Widdermaking Sly," I said, "your interest, as you put it, in ole Lillian ain't no concern to me. Ole Lillian throwed me outa the house, a-shooting at me as I went, and I figger that me and her is quits for good. So whatever she does is her business and none of mine."

The truth of the matter was that I had a couple a good strong reasons for wanting ole Sly to stick around. One a them reasons was Lillian. I really and truly liked what was a-going on between them two, 'cause if it was to persist, that would mean that Lillian was for sure all done with me, and I didn't want to have no more attachments with her. I didn't want her changing her mind and trying to get her clutches back into me. The other reason was that there was so many people in Asininity a-wanting Sly to leave, and I had said that he could stay, so the longer he stayed, and I was a-showing them that it was my word what meant something around our town, the better it was making me feel.

"Barjack," Sly said, "if you really mean that, then would you consent to giving Lillian a divorce?"

"A dee-vorce?" I said. Hell, I hadn't even thought of nothing like that, but of course, a fine gentleman like Sly would. "Well, hell, if that's what she wants, then we'll take keer of it right away. I'll go over and see ole Peester about it first thing in the morning. I reckon he can take keer of that all right. I'll go over and see him about it first thing, on one condition."

"What's that, Barjack?" he said.

"I want you to go over there with me," I said. "There's another little matter that I want to kind of finish up with that little runt, and I need you along to make it work just right."

"I'll go with you," he said. "Certainly."

"All right, then," I said. "It's settled, and I think we had ought to have a drink on that."

"I agree," Sly said.

I poured us each another one, and he wasn't quite so cautious with this one as he had been with his first one. 'Course, this here was more than just my second one. I had drunk me a few while he sipped on that first one. I was beginning to feel pretty good too. Chester Filbert walked in just then, and it tuck me a couple of seconds for the sight of him to really soak into my brain, 'cause he was a-carrying a six-gun in his right hand. He walked straight at the table where I was a-setting with ole Sly, and he raised that gun up and aimed it right smack at Sly's chest.

"You grave digger," Chester said, "I'm tired of waiting. I'm here to kill you."

"If you think you can pull that trigger faster than I can pull mine," Sly said, "go on and try it. I have a Colt Peacemaker under the table, cocked and aimed right at your belly button."

"I don't believe you," Chester said. "You're bluffing."

"Call my bluff," Sly said.

"Chester," I said, "put down that damn gun. Even if

129

you was to kill Sly, which I don't think you can do, then I'll kill you. There ain't no sense in this."

"The sense in it," he said, "is that I'm tired of waiting for him to come after me. I'm tired of waiting, and I mean to finish it right here and now, even if it does kill me. I can't stand it any longer."

"Chester," I said, "if you'll put that gun down right now, we'll forget the whole thing. I won't even throw your ass in jail. Just put the gun down and go on home."

"No," he said. "I'm going to do it."

He thumbed back the hammer on his shooter, and just then ole Bonnie stepped up behind him and swung a half-full bottle of cheap booze about as hard as she could swing, and I know how hard that is from personal experience. That bottle smashed on the back of ole Chester's head, sending pieces of glass and cheap whiskey all over the place, and Chester's face went blank, and his knees buckled, and he fell flat over. God a'mighty damn, I thought for sure she had kilt him.

I jumped up and run over to where he had fell, and I kicked that gun away from him. Sly picked it up and eased the hammer down. The back of ole Chester's head was running blood. I looked up at a table full of citizens not far away, and I said, "A couple of you men carry ole Chester here over to the jail, and one of you go get Doc. Hurry it up, now."

They jumped up to do what I had told them to do, and I walked on back over to where I had been a-setting with Sly. I plopped down again and picked up my tumbler to take me a good long drink. Bonnie come over and set beside me. "You done good, ole gal," I said.

"Thanks," she said. "I didn't want no one getting hurt."

"No one 'cept only ole Chester," I said.

"Well," she said, being defensive-like, "he was the one a-waving the gun around."

"I said you done good, baby," I told her. "Hell, you knocked the crap out of him."

I put a arm around her shoulders and give her a little hug, and I tuck myself another drink.

"Sly," I said, "did you really have your shooter out under the table, or was you a bluffing?"

"I was bluffing, Barjack," he said.

"I'll be damned," I said. "I got to hand it to you, Sly. You're a cool one."

"But you see, Barjack," he said. "There's no end to it."

"There might could be," I said. "Hell, we already knowed about ole Chester. I just never thought the little bastard woulda had the guts to actual point a pistol at you."

"He might have been the one to kill me," Sly said, "if it hadn't been for Miss Boodle here. I sure do want to thank you, ma'am."

Ole Bonnie, she blushed and giggled, and then she said, "Oh, it wasn't nothing, Mister Sly. I'm just glad to of been some help."

"Well," he said, "you certainly were. Without you, someone would surely have been killed here tonight. Maybe more than one. You acted fast, and you did exactly the right thing."

"Yeah, Bonnie," I said. "He's right about all that. Well, I reckon I'd best get my ass over to the jail and see that ole Chester is patched up and locked up and all." I give Bonnie a peck on the cheek, and then I drained my tumbler before standing up. "I'll be back here in just a bit, sweet thing," I said, and I headed on over to my marshaling office.

Chapter Eleven

Well, I never stayed up too late that night, it being my first night back home and all after a couple of days away, and me and ole Bonnie had ourselfs a hell of a reunion, if you know what I mean. Since I was in bed so early, why, just natural I was up and around early the next morning. I had me a breakfast of steak and eggs right there in the Hooch House, and pretty soon, here come ole Sly back from his regular breakfast over at the White Owl. He come right over and set down with me.

"Lillian was very happy at the news," he said. "I want to thank you again."

"Oh," I said, "you mean about the dee-vorce and all."

"Yes," he said.

I didn't know whether to be thrilled and overjoyed or kinda hurt by the news that ole Lillian was very happy about getting herself unhitched from me. I was feeling pretty good about it my own self, so I decided to be thrilled and overjoyed that she was tickled over it too.

"Just let me finish this here coffee," I said, "and we'll take us a little walk over to ole Peester's pettifogging office."

"Sure," said Sly.

Well, ole Peester like to of messed his britches whenever he seen who it was I was a-bringing in to see him, but I told him to just set still and shut up and listen. He set back, all right, but he was some tense, I can tell you that.

"First thing," I said, "I want you to do me up a dee-vorce from ole Lillian. She's agreeable to it, so there won't be no problems."

"There will be the problems of property settlement," Peester said. "You and Mrs. Barjack own a home and a business jointly. That will have to be settled."

"Mr. Mayor," said ole Sly, "Mrs. Barjack, with my help, would like to buy her husband's share of both the home and the business. I'm sure we can agree on a fair price."

He give me a look when he said that, and I nodded. "We can do that for sure," I said. "Now, what other problems do you see a-looming up in fronta you so you can charge more money for this here deal?"

"There's the matter of custody of the child," Peester said.

"I ain't going to fight her over that," I said. "There ain't no problem. Now, can you get this thing did right away?"

"Well," Peester said, "yes, I suppose I can, but are

you absolutely sure of this? Is Mrs. Barjack sure this is what she wants?"

"Me and ole Sly here can both guarantee you that," I said, "but if you need her own word for it, why, hell, we'll send her on over here to see you."

"That would be good," Peester said. "Is that all?"

"No, it ain't," I said. "You been a-shaking in your shoes ever since ole Sly here come to town. You even advised me to break the damn law a time or two. You been acting in such a way that the only thing I can figger is that you're just in the same boat as them others what was so upset about Sly being here. You figgered that he come here special just only to kill you. Am I right about that?"

"Well, I—"

He went on a-blubbering and stammering and never said nothing to get a handle on, so I just interrupted him. "Now, the way I got it figgered," I said, "is that you're a-skeered that either ole Singletree or his missus, what was her name? Agnes? You're a-skeered that one of them two or maybe that there Jonsey hired ole Sly here. Am I on target so far?"

"Barjack, I, well, yes," he said.

"Now Mr. Sly," I said, "have you ever met a man by the name of Singletree?"

"I have not," Sly said.

"Have you ever met Agnes Singletree?" I said.

"Never," said Sly. "I assure you, I'd remember that name."

"And what about Jonsey?" I said.

"No," he said.

135

"Then you ain't come to town with it in your head to kill ole Peester here?" I said.

"I never heard of Mr. Peester before I came to town," Sly said. "Further, as I told you before, Marshal, I didn't come here to kill anyone. I came here for a much-needed rest."

"Now, Peester," I said, "did you hear all that?"

Peester nodded his head up and down real fast and silly looking. "Yes. Yes," he said.

"Do you believe that Mr. Sly here is a-lying to you?" I asked him.

"Oh no. Oh no," Peester said. "I believe what he said."

"Then for once and for all," I said, "are you a-going to relax and just let me do the marshaling job and stop hounding me and stop worrying about what Mr. Sly is a-doing here?"

"Yes, Barjack," Peester said. "I promise."

" 'Cause in the first place," I said, "he ain't lying to you. He ain't after you. In the second place, if I get any more trouble outa you on this here matter or any other matter, I just might be tempted to reopen a old case that had something to do with ole Singletree and his Agnes. You get my meaning?"

"I understand you, Barjack," Peester said. "Believe me, everything's all right. I'm sure that I've come to a clear understanding of the presence of Mr. Sly in our community, and I have no problem with it whatsoever. None. Furthermore, I'll get to work on these divorce papers right away."

"That's good," I said. "We'll send ole Lillian on over to visit with you."

"Yes," he said. "Please do."

As I turned to head out the door, Sly touched the brim of his hat. "Thank you, Mr. Mayor," he said.

Me and ole Sly walked on out into the street, and Sly give me a look and a grin. "Barjack," he said, "I've never known anyone quite like you. You handled that all very neatly."

"You just got to know how to deal with ole Peester," I said. "That's all. You want to stop by the White Owl and tell Lillian to get her ass on over to Peester's office?"

"I'll do that," he said, "happily, but I won't phrase it in exactly that way."

Well, I didn't have no reason to see her, likely never would again, so I said toodle-oo to ole Sly and headed my ass back on over toward the Hooch House. And I was a-thinking as I walked along how ever'thing had turned out just about damn near perfect. For one thing, I had final got ole Peester all shut up and at my mercy, since I knowed about them Singletree stories. It didn't make no nevermind that I didn't know which story was the truth. It was enough that I knowed about them. And not only did I know, but he knowed that I knowed, and on top of all that, I believed that I really did have him final convinced that he weren't in no danger from ole Sly.

Then there was all of them others what had tuck Sly's appearance in Asininity so hard. It did seem like as if they had all been calmed down or locked up or kilt, and it looked like there weren't going to be no more trouble along them lines neither. But the best of all was the wonderful fact that my Lillian and ole Sly had fell for each other in a real big way, and that was a-going to get

Lillian offa my back for once and good. I tell you what. I didn't believe that I had a worry in the whole entire world that day.

Oh, I was going to have to go to court over to the county seat in a few days, but that weren't nothing but a minor inconvenience. I'd have to go over there with Sly and Happy and Bonnie, 'cause they was all important witnesses in that there case. We'd have to tell the judge what we seen and how ever'thing happened and all, but I didn't see no problems with none of that. Like I said, I figgered it to be a minor annoyance is all.

I seen ole Happy walking along toward the jailhouse, and I give him a smile and a wave. I started on over to the Hooch House. I didn't know what kinda company I might have in there. It was early. Bonnie would still be in bed, and I weren't about to bother her that early. I weren't quite ready for my next flying lesson. I thought that maybe ole Sly would come on over and join me after he had walked Lillian to Peester's office.

I went on inside the Hooch House and found Aubrey a-serving a beer to a cowboy on his day off. I wasn't ready to start in on my day's drunk, so I told Aubrey to get me some coffee, and I went on over to my favorite table and set my ass down. He brung me my coffee in just a bit. I drunk two cups before ole Sly come on in and set down with me. Aubrey brung him some coffee and then went away to leave us alone.

"Barjack," said Sly, "I want to tell you my plans."

"Ain't none of my business," I said.

"I want to tell you anyway, if you don't mind," Sly said.

"Well, all right," I said, "if that's the way you feel about it, go on ahead."

"As soon as your divorce is final," he said, "Lillian and I mean to be married. I intend to be the best stepfather I can be for the boy. I'm going to give Lillian the money to buy your share of the house and the White Owl from you, and then I mean to settle right here in Asininity. Do you have any problem with any of that?"

"The only thing I might could have a problem with," I said, "is letting the White Owl stay on in business and me not making no profit from it. I been real careful about that sort of thing here. You mighta noticed that there ain't no place in town you can get whiskey or beer 'cept from me. But in this case, since it'll be you and Lillian, and since in a way I will be a making a profit from it, I reckon it won't bother me none at all."

"You don't mind," Sly said, "if I marry your ex-wife and go right on living here in the same town with you?"

"Hell, no," I said. "I ain't got no one to drink with here other than Happy and Bonnie and now you. I don't want you going nowhere."

He seemed to relax considerable, and he grinned wide at me. "Thank you, Barjack," he said. "I have another question for you."

"Shoot," I said, and then it come to me that was maybe not the best way to answer the Widdermaker, but I had done said it, so I let it go.

"What are you planning to do with that man over in your jail?" he asked me.

"Aw, hell," I said, "I figger I'll just let him set there till they send word over from the county seat when we got to go back over yonder for the trial of them others.

139

Then I'll just carry him along with us and turn him over and make the charges on him then."

"I've been thinking about him," Sly said. "Why don't you and I go have a talk with him?"

"You ain't thinking we had maybe oughta let him go or something like that are you?" I said.

"I don't know," he said. "Let's have a talk with him."

"Well, all right," I said. "When you want to do that?"

"Anything wrong with right now?" he said.

We finished the coffee we had in our cups and got up and walked on over to the jailhouse. Happy was a-setting behind my desk warming the seat of my big chair with his skinny ass and propping his feet up on my desk. He jumped up when he seen me a-coming and moved on over to his own little chair. I thought about chewing his ass out, but I decided to let it go this time.

"Happy," I said, "why don't you go on over to the Hooch House or someplace for a little break. Me and ole Sly here are fixing to have us a talk with ole Chester."

Happy run on out the door, likely feeling lucky that I hadn't said nothing to him about setting in my chair, and me and ole Sly each grabbed a chair and pulled them over by the bars to set down.

"Chester," I said, "how you feeling in there?"

"My head hurts," Chester said. He looked at Sly. "What's he doing here?"

"Well, he ain't here to kill you," I said.

"What're you going to do with me?" Chester asked me.

"I ain't for sure about that," I said. "Mr. Sly here wants to talk with you. Maybe what you have to say will have something to do with the answer to your question there."

"Mr. . . . Filbert is it?" Sly said.

"That's right," said Chester, looking real cautious and suspicious.

"Mr. Filbert," Sly went on, "first off, I want to assure you that I did not come here to kill you. I never heard your name before I came to town. Now, I'd like to ask you just who it is that you think might have wanted you dead badly enough to have hired me."

Chester looked at the floor and never said nothing.

"Listen, you silly little bastard," I said, "Sly here is giving you a chance even after you went and tried to kill him. If you know what's good for you, you'll cooperate a little here."

"You mean if I tell you, you'll let me go?" Chester said.

"I ain't making no rash promises," I said, "but if you don't tell us, I might come back in here after a while all by my own self and beat the crap outa you till you do tell me."

"It's my brother," Chester said.

"Well, now," I said, "how come your own brother would want you dead?"

"Back east," said Chester, "our paw had a farm. Well, when Paw died, me and Ezra, we inherited the place together. Well, Ezra wanted to farm it, but I didn't. I just wanted to get away from the farm. I hated it. I wanted to sell, and we had a big fight over it. Well, I packed up my clothes and went to town, and I sold my half and took off. I used that money to get myself set up out here with the store and all. I figured all these years Ezra had it in for me, and when Sly here came to town, it came to me that Ezra had finally found me."

"That's it?" I said.

"That's it," he said.

"Well," said Sly, "I've never met your brother. I've never heard of him until now. I assure you that I did not come to town looking for you."

"Do you believe that, Chester?" I asked.

"Yeah, I guess so," Chester said. "I guess I've just been a fool. Feeling guilty all these years—I guess it just made me kind of crazy."

"Mr. Filbert," said Sly, "have you got enough money to pay your brother back for what you did to him?"

"Well, yeah," said Chester. "I guess I have."

"Then I suggest that you write him a letter of apology," Sly said, "and send him the money. That would ease your conscience, and it might even reconcile you with your brother."

"Yeah," said Chester, of a sudden brightening up some, like as if such a simpleminded idee had never even come into his head before. "Yeah. I could do that."

"Barjack," Sly said. "May I have a word with you in private?"

Me and ole Sly got up and walked out the door to stand on the sidewalk there, just the two of us.

"What is it?" I said.

"I know that you have a case against Mr. Filbert," Sly said, "and I know that I can't just say I won't press charges, and you'll have to let him go, but I'd rather see him go free than go to trial. Of course, it's up to you."

"Hell, Sly," I said, "you're the one he wanted to shoot

a hole in. If you want me to turn him loose, I reckon I don't give a damn. I'll turn him loose."

We went back inside, and ole Chester, he looked real anxious 'cause we had give him a glimmer of hope. We walked on back over there to the bars of the cell where Chester was locked up.

"Chester," I said, "Mr. Sly here don't want to press no charges on you. I could go on and do it myself, and likely I had ought to do just that. You did try to kill a man, and right in front of my eyes, too. But I'm going along with what Mr. Sly here wants, and he wants you to go free. But first, I want you to assure me that you ain't going to pull no more fool stunts like what you done before."

"I promise you, Barjack," Chester said. "I promise you that I won't go gunning for Mr. Sly or anyone else ever again. I realize what a fool I acted. It won't happen again. And Mr. Sly, I want to apologize for my actions and thank you for what you're doing for me. If I get out of here, I'll write that letter to my brother and send him the money. I promise you. I promise you, and I thank you."

"All right, Chester," I said. "That's enough promising. Just shut up now and count your goddamn blessings."

I walked over to my desk and got out my keys. Then I walked over to the cell door and unlocked it and opened the door.

"Get on outa here and go home," I said. "And don't never do nothing to make me put you in here again."

"I won't," he said. "I won't. I promise you."

"Shut up, Chester," I said. "My promise to you is that if you ever make me come after you again, I won't just stop at locking you up. I'll mash you up real good first. Maybe even kill you to save me some trouble. Now, get on outa here."

Chester, he practical run out the door. I never seen a man so anxious to get out of a place as he was. I looked over at ole Sly.

"Well," I said, "I don't know if we done the right thing or not."

"I believe we did," Sly said. "I've seen what my presence in a town does to people. I don't believe he'll ever do anything like that again. Besides, who would you get to run the store in town if you sent him to prison?"

"Hell," I said, "that's a good question. Ole Peester would likely find a way to get his hands on the property and turn hisself a good profit from it. Well, I think this calls for a drink. What do you say?"

"For me," Sly said, "just one."

I got the bottle and the tumblers outa my desk drawer and poured one for each of us. We was just tipping them back when ole Happy come in a-waving a piece of paper in his hand.

"Wire come in for you, Barjack," he said.

"Well," I said, "give it here. I s'pose you've done read it."

He handed me the paper and kinda ducked his head, and I knowed that he had read it all right. I looked it over real quick-like. It was from ole Dick Custer over to the county seat, and it told me to bring all my witnesses and be over for the trial in just two days from then. I told Sly, and then I started over to the Hooch House to tell Bonnie. Sly and Happy walked along with me.

Chapter Twelve

Ole Lillian never got herself called over to the trial, even though she actual was both a witness and a participant, but we just never did put her name into the story. I knowed she wouldn't want to leave her precious White Owl either closed up or in the hands of anyone else, and besides that, I figgered that we'd have a easy enough time of it at the trial and more fun at night without her. So we had just about got back to the Hooch House when ole Sly stopped me. He give a kinda longing look over toward the White Owl, and he said, "Barjack, I'd like to go tell Lillian about the trial dates."

"Oh, sure," I said. "Go right on ahead, then. Me and ole Happy, we can go on ahead and tell ole Bonnie."

"There's one more thing, Barjack," Sly said.

"What's that?" I asked him.

"Well," he said, "now that we're all agreed—that is,

you and me and Lillian—and now that the divorce and the ensuing wedding are both decided on, do you think it would be proper, that is, would it be all right if I visited Lillian in the parlor this evening?"

"The parlor?" I said. "You mean go on into the house?"

"Yes," he said.

"Why, hell yes," I said. "You can visit her all night in the bedroom if you take a mind to. I sure as hell don't give a damn, and it ain't none of my business no more." I wondered how many times I was going to have to say that to him before it for real soaked into his head.

"I assure you," he said, "I won't do that. Not until after the wedding."

Ole Sly turned and headed on for the White Owl, and me and Happy went on to the Hooch House. We went inside and found ole Bonnie a-leaning up against the bar with her big titties just a-laying there on it. She had her a drink. I walked on up to her and said, "Bring your drink on over to the table, sweet butt, and tell ole Aubrey to fetch me and Happy my bottle and two glasses."

She done that, and the three of us was all settled in pretty soon. I told Bonnie that we all had to go on over to the county seat, and I told her when.

"What about the Hooch House?" she said.

"Hell," I said. "It'll be all right. Aubrey can run things well enough, and you got some other gals working upstairs. It likely won't even miss us. Besides, we'll make it like a little vacation, you and me. We'll get us a room over there, and there won't be no one come a-banging on it to call me out for no marshaling business, nor bothering you about bar or gal business."

She hugged my arm then and smiled up into my face and said, "Oh, that'll be nice, Barjack."

"But there'll be the trial," Happy said.

"Well, yeah," I said. "That there's the reason we're going over there, but we'll go to the trial and do what we have to do, and then whenever the trial's did for the day, we'll be free. Hell, you ain't even s'posed to talk about what's going on in a trial 'lessen you're right there in the courtroom and the trial's a-going on and you're answering questions the lawyers or the judge is asking you direct. So our evenings is all going to be free and fun. And on the town of Asininity."

"You mean I ain't got to spend none of my own money at all?" Happy asked me.

"Not a cent," I said. "We'll get our ride over there and back, we'll get our rooms, we'll get three meals a day and all the whiskey we want." I leaned over a little towards ole Happy, and I added, "Hell, boy, we might even get you a good whore each night."

I figgered it was good politics to stop short of telling him about the whore I had got me over there the last time, what with Bonnie a-setting right there and hanging on to my arm and all. So we talked on like that about all the fun we was going to have us over there at the county seat, and we drunk up a whole bunch of whiskey, and by and by, here come ole Sly back from Lillian's place. I figgered that he for sure had gone in and set with her and visited real polite-like and never even got close to no bed. Hell, I bet he never even stuck his hand inside her dress nowhere, he was such a gentleman. Anyhow, he come over and set with us, and by damn, he ordered up a whiskey. I reckon he was final real good and relaxed and felt, like I did, that all the troubles in Asininity was over with and did.

I had Aubrey fetch him over a glass, and I filled it outa my own bottle. He didn't just sip on it the way he usual done, neither. He drank it on down. I poured us all another one, and we was having us a grand old time there. That's for sure. Hell, I thought, whenever it's time for me to kick on over, I hope it's right here and just like this. I don't want to get my ass shot to death, nor hanged, nor get sick and cough to death for three or four weeks, nor fall outa the sky a-trying to fly. Just take a drink of good whiskey and fall over dead right smack in the middle of a laugh with good friends all around. That's the way to go.

I decided to tell my good friends just what I was a-thinking about, and I did, but ole Bonnie, she said that I was being morbid and told me to shut up. I looked over at Sly, and I said, "Was I being morbid, Sly? I coulda been, 'cause I ain't real sure just what the hell that means." Bonnie decided to change the subject real quick-like, and she said, "Barjack, we'll have to make sure you got a clean suit and all before we head over to the county seat."

"Hell," I said, "ole Dick Custer won't know the difference."

"I will," she said, "and it's going to be our vacation, ain't it?"

"Well, hell," I said, "let's get me two clean suits ready, and three or four clean shirts. Maybe even a change of long johns and some fresh socks. What do you say to all that?"

"Barjack," said Sly, "do you anticipate any problems at the trial?"

"Nary a one," I said. "Hell, what could it be? I'm the law over here, and I'm the number-one witness. Well, me and ole Happy here. It's clean obvious what tuck place out there at that elum tree, and we got the witnesses to back it all up. Hell, if need be we could call in even more: ole Lillian, Aubrey there. Naw. There ain't going to be no problems."

I didn't want no more serious talk, on account of it was starting in to get kinda loud in the place. Since we had come in earlier, the place had begun to fill up. We was doing a whale of a business of a sudden that night. The crowd was keeping ole Aubrey jumping. Bonnie final got up and went over to the bar to give him a hand. Right the next table to me and Happy and ole Sly was a table full of cowboys, and they had done got their ass plenty drunk, and then just outa nowhere, one of the bastards looked over at me, and he hollered out, "Hey, Barjack, why don't you go up there and fly for us again tonight?"

"Well, why don't I just kick your ass plumb out into the middle of the street?" I said.

"Barjack," said Happy, "take it easy."

"You go up them stairs with me," I said to that cowboy, "and we'll just see which one of us goes a-flying."

"Take it easy, Charlie," another cowboy said. "He's the damn law."

"Ah, hell," Charlie said, "I know who the hell he is. I'd stomp the crap out of him if it weren't for that badge."

Well, goddamn it, that done it for me. I stood straight

up outa my chair, and I plucked that marshal's badge right offa my vest. I slapped it down on the table in front of Happy, and I said, "Happy, watch that thing for me, and don't you nor no one else go interfering with me and this dumbass cowboy."

I seen Sly give Happy a look, and Happy just give a shrug. The cowboy stood up and stepped toward me, and I said, "Hold on there, you dumbass." He stopped still, and I unbuckled my gunbelt and put it on the table. He tuck the hint, and he done the same thing. "This here is going to be a clean and a fair fight," I said, and just as he was looking up from putting his gun down, I whopped him up along the side of his head with a right, just as hard as I could swing. I heard Bonnie scream out at me from over behind the bar. "Barjack!"

Well, ole Charlie fell back onto the table what he had been a-setting at, and his buddies' drinks all spilled. They went to cussing, and Charlie, he straightened his ass up a-rubbing the side of his head. I hit him again. One of his buddies stood up then and jumped me from behind, and I give him a elbow in the gut. He come loose from me all right. But by then, Charlie had recovered some, and he had his fists up ready to do battle. I put mine up, too, and then I kicked him in the shinbone. He hollered and went to hopping around on one leg, and so I slugged him again and that punch knocked him over on his ass. I give him a kick or two in the ribs, and then all his pards jumped up.

Well, whenever they done that, why, ole Happy and ole Sly both come up outa their chairs, too. Happy come up swinging a chair, and he tuck one cowboy outa the fight right then. Sly commenced gentlemanly fisticuffs

150

with another one, and the poor boy didn't hardly know what Sly was a-doing nor how to deal with it, and Sly was a-getting cutting blows to the bastard's face with almost ever' punch.

I had one of them come at me, and he managed to get a good one to my jaw. It stunned me somewhat, but it never knocked me offa my feet, and I hit him back, but then ole Charlie come up offa the floor, and he come over to help this one out. Sly and Happy each one had a man they was fighting, so there weren't no one to take the extry one offa me, and there I was with two of them a-swinging at me.

Just then there come a hell of a roar, and ever'one stopped the fighting and turned to look toward the bar, and there was ole Bonnie a-holding a smoking shotgun. "Knock it off," she roared, and I ain't sure whether the shotgun blast or her voice was the loudest. By God, we all done what she said, and we was dusting off our clothes and picking up hats and such, and Bonnie come out from behind the bar and right over to where we was at. She was still a-holding that shotgun, and she give poor ole Charlie a hard look.

"Take your buddies and get outa here," she said.

"Aw, Bonnie," I said, "hell, it was me what started the fight. Let them stay."

She looked at me, then back at Charlie and at his pals. "I don't want no more fighting," she said.

"It's all over," I said, and I give ole Charlie a look. He grinned and held his hand out to me, and I shuck it.

"No more fighting, ma'am," he said. "I promise you."

"Well," Bonnie said, "see that you don't then," and she walked on back to the bar and put away the gun.

Charlie still had aholt of my hand, and he was a-grinning right in my face.

"Barjack," he said, "you're a tough son of a bitch. It's been a pleasure."

"Hell," I said, "whyn't you and your friends come on over and set with us? Let me buy you all a drink."

They done just that, and they all shuck hands with Happy and with Sly and interduced theirselves, and you should oughta have seen their faces whenever they found out who ole Sly really was.

"Goddamn," said the one cowboy, "and me trading punches with the honest-to-God Widowmaker."

Sly laughed. "I never killed a man for that," he said.

We all had us some good laughs about the fight what we had never finished and the way ole Bonnie like to skeered the crap outa all of us, and I used up two more bottles of my good whiskey providing the drinks all around the table. Then I had me a startling thought. I recalled the morning that ole Bonnie had give me my first flying lesson, and then I thought about her a-being called in to the trial early of a morning. I wondered who it would be would have to wake her ass up for that duty, and it come into my head that I would be the one what got chose for that unpleasant chore.

"Hey, fellas," I said, "I got something important I got to do."

I got up and made my way over to the bar and got Bonnie's attention. When she come over to me, I tuck her arm and made her go outside with me so we could talk over all the noise what was going on inside.

"Bonnie," I said, "them trials start at eight in the morning."

I didn't for real know that, but I just wanted to make sure I impressed on her that she was going to have to wake up early whenever we went over there for the trial. She looked genuine horrified.

"Eight?" she said. "You mean eight o'clock in the morning?"

"And if you ain't there on time," I said, "they might just throw your ass in jail for being contemptuous of the court."

"What's that mean?" she said.

"I ain't sure," I said, "but they'll do it just the same."

"Barjack," she said, "what am I going to do?"

"There's only one thing you can do," I said, "and you got to start right now."

"Tell me," she said.

"You got to go upstairs right now," I said, "and put your ass to bed and do your damndest to go to sleep. Then you got to let me or Aubrey or someone wake you up a little more earlier in the morning than what you're used to, and you got to promise you won't try to kill the one what gets assigned that dangerous chore. Then tomorry night you go to bed even earlier, and you get up earlier the next morning. Thataway, you might get through the trial all right. Whenever it's all over, why, hell, you can go right back to the way you always done before."

"Oh, God," she said, "this is awful. Well, all right. I'll try it that way. But Barjack, Aubrey's real busy in there. If I go on upstairs, will you help him out behind the bar?"

"Sure thing, sweet britches," I said. "You go on and take your ass to bed. I'll watch over things down here."

Well, she went on upstairs, and I hoped that my little plan would work out. I sure didn't want her throwing my ass down no stairways over at the county seat. I went on back into the bar and seen that Aubrey was for sure hustling them drinks up as fast as he could go. I made my way back to the table where Happy and Sly and Charlie and them other cowhands was still a-setting and a-drinking my whiskey, and I set back down with them. I found my tumbler what I had left there, and I filled her up again and had me a good long drink. I guess I had come back inside right smack in the middle of some kinda conversation, 'cause a cowboy was saying to Happy, "I sure do hope that you nor Barjack throws my ass in jail and Mr. Sly here don't kill me."

"Aw, none of that ain't going to happen," Happy said. "Leastwise, not on account of what went on in here to-night."

"It just makes me kinda nervous," the cowhand said, "to get into a fight with a marshal and his deputy and the famous Widowmaker all at the same time. You know, ole Charlie here, he never was too bright."

"You son of a bitch," Charlie said.

"See what I mean?" the cowboy said. "Listen to him talking to me like that. He knows I can whip him. Hell, I done it three times already."

"Well," Charlie said, "you might just have to make it four."

I guessed that ole cowboy was right about what he had just said. That Charlie weren't too bright. He did have him a good hard jaw, though. I had found out that much by hitting on it. Just about then, ole Happy, who as you likely already know is kinda slow hisself in his thinking sometimes, musta noticed that Bonnie had done left the place. He said, "Barjack, where's Bonnie?"

"I had to start her in on training," I said, taking me a long drink from my tumbler.

"Training?" Happy said. "For what?"

"Hell," I said, "for getting up early to make it to the trial on time."

Chapter Thirteen

Well, the three of us witnesses and ole Sly, the victim, we unloaded our tired asses offa the stage over to the county seat, and they already had rooms a-waiting for us in the hotel there. The trial was scheduled to start the next morning at ten, and whenever she heard that, ole Bonnie give me a real dirty look, but anyhow Happy and Bonnie and Sly all said they had to get theirselves some sleep so they'd be ready to go in the morning. I went on over to the nearest saloon to have me a few drinks of good whiskey before I retired for the night. I seen ole Dick Custer in there, and me and him had us a couple drinks together. I opined as how the trial had oughta be short and sweet, and he told me that I was right, it had oughta be that for sure. Only thing was, he said, that them boys had got theirselves ole Rance Stinger for their defense lawyer, and he was a slick one.

"Be careful what you say, Barjack," he warned me.

Well, it turned out the next day that ole Custer was right, sort of. Ole Stinger did his damndest to lay ever'thing off on ole Sly. These men, Stinger said, was all good citizens, and knowing that their beloved community was harboring a notorious killer, a man what murdered for money, and them knowing that their own town marshal was a-siding with him, getting drunk with him, even sharing his wife with him, why, they just natural decided to take the law into their own hands. He purt near had that jury convinced, I believe.

But the other side got me and then Happy and then Bonnie on the stand, and the three of us, whenever you put our whole stories together, told them the whole truth. I told them that all the citizens of Asininity was skeered to death whenever they heard who had stopped over in our town, but I said that I had visited with ole Sly and had determined that he weren't in town to do no killing. I had also did my research and knowed that he weren't wanted for no crimes, and I assured them that he hadn't committed no crimes in my town. I even told them as how he had stopped a long-standing feud, and how two men had come a-gunning for him, and he hadn't killed neither one of them even though he could of did it real easy and total legal as self-defense.

Then Happy told how that mob had come after Sly and just what they had did to get him, including knocking ole Happy silly and him the town depitty marshal. He told the whole story about how all that come about, and Bonnie did too. In the end they didn't have no choice but what to find them fine upstanding citizens, each and all, guilty as hell of attempted murdering and

157

partial responsible for the death of ole Marty Bodene. Well, the judge, it was ole Hard-nose Harrison, he dismissed the court till the next morning whenever we was all to show up again to hear the sentencing, so we went out to get us some supper.

Now, if you know about the time whenever I sent them Bensons off to the pen and then they got out later and come a-looking to kill me for it, you might be a-thinking that I was worried about the time when this bunch would get out. Well, I weren't. You see, they wasn't hardcases like them Bensons had been. 'Cept for that one fool thing they done, they really was good citizens, and they was all genuine ashamed for what they had did. I didn't have no worries about none of them coming around later looking to get even. Hell, none of them wouldn't hardly even look no one in the face during the whole entire trial.

Well, we had us a steak dinner, and then we all went on over to the saloon and ordered us up some good whiskey, me and Happy and Bonnie and ole Sly, and we found us a table and set together to drink. I looked around and tuck stock of what kinda folks was in that place. The county seat was some bigger than Asininity, and the saloon there was packed a mite tighter than what the Hooch House usual got, even though I had fixed it up so that the Hooch House was the only place to go for a drink in our town. Well, might' near the only one, the only other'n being the White Owl Supper Club what was owned by my wife. But that was all fixing to change, as you well know. Anyhow, I noticed a few pretty tough-looking customers in the place, one bunch in particular what was all a-setting together that seemed to be eyeballing us some. I figgered it was just 'cause we was knowed to be in town for the trial. Well, by and by ole Sly excused hisself and headed for his room. I figgered he was just being his old cautious self, since we was over there in another town what he was not familiar with and so not total comfortable in.

After a while ole Bonnie got up to go out back, and me and Happy set there a-drinking and a-talking about the trial and about that bunch we was fixing to send up. I don't know how much time had went by, but then I heard ole Bonnie's voice. There weren't no mistaking it.

"Get your hands offa me, you son of a bitch," she hollered.

I jumped up and looked around and seen her take a swing at a poor ole cowhand what was about half drunk and had likely spotted ole Bonnie for what she was and had made some kinda proposal to her, I reckon. She had tuck offense at it, I guess, likely 'cause me and her was so tight, and she had done quit taking on customers again so that I would be her only lover. Well, now, I knowed the poor ole cowhand had made a honest mistake, but then, Bonnie was my woman, so what was I to do? I went on over there and knocked him on his ass.

He musta had some friends in that place, 'cause someone hit me over the head with a chair just then, and the next thing I knowed the whole damn saloon had become a battlefield. I know I knocked out some teeth, and I think I busted a arm, but about the third time I got hit on the back of the head, I went down and blacked out. I woke up the next morning in a jail cell. My head was hurting like hell. As I slowly woke up and looked around, I seen that Happy was in there with me, and ole

Bonnie was a-sleeping it off in the next door cell. By and by, ole Custer come around.

"Barjack," he said, "trouble follows you around like a faithful dog. I'm going to let you three out of here, because the trial's starting up in just a few minutes. Then, as a favor to a fellow law officer, I'm not filing any charges—if you'll get out of town right away. There's a stage leaving at noon. The trial ought to be done by then. I want you and all your friends on that stage."

"We'll be on the son of a bitch," I said. "I sure don't want to hang around here no longer than I have to. You got a damn unfriendly town here, you know that?"

Well, he let me and ole Happy out, and somehow he got Bonnie woke up and outa her cell without getting tossed through the air, and the three of us headed over to the courthouse. We met Sly there, and we all went in and set together. Ole Custer was right. It didn't take long. Ole Hard-nose sent them boys all off to the pen for a few years and then dismissed the court.

"Well," I said, as we was a-standing up to leave, "we got to be on the noon stage, so let's all go get our stuff together and be ready."

I didn't give them no more details just how come we had to be on that stage, and they didn't ask. We walked out the front door of the courthouse, and the four of us was standing in a row, and I seen that mean-ass bunch I had noticed in the saloon. They was standing shoulder to shoulder out in the middle of the street facing us. I swear what I remember of what happened next is real hazy and kinda dreamy-like, but I heard one of them bastards yell out, "There he is," and then I seen all their hands go for guns. Outa the corner of my eye, I seen ole Sly whip out his own Colt, but after that I don't know nothing 'cept hearing gun blasts and feeling them damn pieces of lead slamming into my body. I don't know how many times I got hit.

Well, I guess the son of a bitches damn near killed me. The next thing I know is I come out of it a-hurting like hell, sore all over like I'd been beat up and down with a stick, and hungry as a bear right after hibernating. I was in a strange bed, but what weren't strange was ole Bonnie was setting right there by the bed. Whenever I opened my eyeballs, she commenced to squealing.

"Oh, Barjack," she said. "Barjack. God, I was afraid they'd killed you. Oh, God, you're awake."

"Yeah, hell," I said, "and I'm hungry, too."

Well, she got me a big bowl of some kinda stew right away, and she got me some coffee. I told her I wanted some whiskey, but she said the doc wouldn't allow that. She told me I was still over to the county seat laying right in the same bed they had first brung me to whenever I got blowed away. After I had et me some of that there stew and drunk me a couple cups of coffee, things started in to coming back into my head, and I asked her about ole Sly.

"He's doing a little better than you, Barjack," she said. "He got outa bed yesterday, but he was shot up pretty bad too. Them Jaspers like to of killed the both of you."

"Jaspers?" I said.

"That's who they was," she said. "The sheriff told me. There was seven of them. They was after Mister Sly, but you happened to be standing next to him is all, so they went for you too. The sheriff, he killed one of them, and Sly, he got one before they brung him down. One of them's wounded and setting over there in the county jail."

"That leaves four," I said.

"Yeah," she said. "They got away."

Well, I guess I kinda faded out again, and I think that for the next several days it was like that, you know, kinda in and out, and when I final really come to my senses and could get up and down sorta by my own self, why, ole Bonnie told me I'd been laid up there in bed in that county seat for nigh onto two weeks. Ole Sly, he'd come back around and got up in just over a week. Either he was a tougher son of a bitch than me or he weren't hit as bad. I ain't sure which, but if he weren't hit as bad as me that sure as hell weren't fair, 'cause them Jaspers was really a-trying to kill him, not me.

Somehow neither Bonnie nor Happy had even got hit with all them bullets a-flying, and Bonnie had told Happy to get his ass on back to Asininity and keep his eye on things over there. Well, with me final coming back around, the three of us, me and Bonnie and ole Sly, we packed up our things and loaded our ass onto the next stage. Ole Custer was sure glad to see us go, too. He told me just before we left that he had sent out wires on them Jaspers, and I just kinda grunted at that. He also said the judge had give that wounded one a speedy trial, and they was a-fixing to hang his ass. Bonnie lugged all of my bags as well as her own out to the stage. She wouldn't have me toting nothing heavier than just the clothes on my back.

That was the roughest stage ride I have ever tuck, and

a course it was all 'cause of them bullet holes in me. I was still sore all over my whole entire body. But I was glad to be getting home anyhow. Whenever we rolled into Asininity, ole Happy, he come a-running. "Barjack," he hollered, "am I glad to see you up and around. I was sure worried about you." And you know what? I believe that he really had been. Then I seen ole Lillian a-standing over on the sidewalk. Sly seen her too, and he walked on over there to where she was a-standing, and they give each other a hug right there for all the world to see. They hadn't never did that before. Out in public like that.

I started in to making my way toward the Hooch House kinda slow and easy, and Sly and Lillian caught up with me. "Barjack," Lillian said, "I'm glad you're all right. I really am." I didn't hardly know what to say to her, so I just kinda nodded and grunted. Then she said, "Our divorce is final, Barjack. I just thought you'd want to know."

"Oh, yeah," I said. "Well, thanks for that there information, Lillian." I tipped my hat kinda like ole Sly mighta did and excused my ass and headed on for the Hooch House. Ole Bonnie had been holding me up by my left arm all this time, and she kept a-doing it all the way on over to our saloon. I weren't sorry for the way things was a-turning out, but the news about the dee-vorce kinda set me back a bit. I guess just 'cause it was a big change in my life, you know. Anyhow, I was pretty quiet all the way till, me and Bonnie was a setting in our own favorite chairs at our own favorite table and our own barkeep, ole Aubrey, was a-running over at us with our favorite drinks.

Damn, I was glad to have that whiskey. I hadn't had none since I'd been blasted all to hell. It sure did taste good. Happy come in and set with us, too, and I said that ever'one had ought to be having a drink with me to celebrate that them bastard Jaspers hadn't killed my ass. Then I pulled myself out a ceegar and lit that up. That was another pleasure that had been kept away from me for about two whole damn weeks. Well, the ceegar made me dizzy, and the drink made me woozy, and I figgered that my inactivity for them two long weeks and what blood I had lost and all had really got me outa shape for the serious things in life. I told Bonnie how I was feeling, and she tuck me upstairs to bed.

Next morning I was up early. 'Course Bonnie weren't, and I didn't dare do nothing about it. I figgered if she was to send me a-flying again, in the shape I was in, it would kill me deader'n hell for sure. I got myself dressed and went down the stairs real slow and easy. Aubrey was at work, and he went to fixing me a breakfast right away. Pretty soon ole Happy come in, and me and him set down together and had our breakfasts there.

"That Sly is sure a gentleman," Happy said.

"How's that?" I said.

"Even with you and Lillian divorced," Happy said, "Sly still wouldn't stay in the house with her last night."

"You a-spying on them, are you?" I said.

"Well, no. Not really," said Happy, "but I seen them walk over to your—to the house last night. I just happened to be out there thataway, and I seen them. That's all."

I went on eating, and Aubrey come over to refill our coffee cups. It sure was good to be home, but I wished that I wasn't feeling so weak. I sure couldn't afford to get no one real mad at me. A good punch to the jaw or to the gut woulda broke me in half.

"Speaking of Sly," I said, "I reckon he's still over at the White Owl?"

"No sir," said Happy. "He had his breakfast, and then he mounted up and rode outa town. I think he's out there practicing up with his six-guns."

I stopped eating on that and just looked at ole Happy for a few seconds. "Getting back in shape, is he?" I said.

"I reckon," Happy said.

I figgered that old Sly was thinking on going after them Jaspers what was still left alive, and damned if I weren't thinking the same thing. I weren't about to let no one get away with doing what they done to me, not if I could help it any. 'Course, they had more than a two-week head start on us by then, and we didn't have no idea where they mighta went to, not even what direction they had rid off in whenever they left outa the county seat that day. Even so, I wanted to go after them, and I knowed that old Sly did too. I figgered we'd team up and go together, unless he had any objections to that plan.

I didn't figger that I'd need to go out and do what he was a-doing, though. I ain't never been what you'd call no gunfighter, and I couldn't see no call in practicing up to get back something what I'd never had in the first place. If you know anything about me at all, you know that facing a man out in the open for a fair gun duel just ain't my style. If I know a man wants to kill me for real and serious, I'd lots rather sneak up behind his ass with a big club, or lay a-waiting for him along the trail with my rifle ready, or something like that. And them kinda tactics don't call for no long hours of practice.

I seen Sly that morning getting close to lunchtime. He come into the Hooch House to go up to his room and clean up and change his clothes before going on over to the White Owl for his lunch, but when he seen me setting there, he come on over to see me.

"How are you doing, Barjack?" he said.

"Not as good as you," I said, "but I'm coming along. I reckon I'll live all right."

"I feel bad about what happened," he said. "Those men wanted me. You just happened to be standing too close by. I promise you, though, they won't get away with it. You know, Barjack, I usually go after a man for money. This will be the first time in my life I'll be going after men out of anger."

"What the hell did they want you for anyhow?" I asked him.

"I killed a brother of theirs," he said. "It's been almost a year ago."

"So you'll be a-going after them?" I said.

"That's what I mean to do," he said.

"Sly," I said, "I want to go along with you. Before you answer me one way or the other, I want you to know that I'll be a-going after them whether you want my company or not."

"I'd be pleased to have your company, Barjack," he said.

"Thanks," I said. "You, uh, you mean to hitch up with ole Lillian before we take off?"

"No," he said. "I've already told her. I don't think it would be fair to her. The wedding will wait until we get back from taking care of this little chore."

I thought, I shoulda knowed that without asking, but I didn't say nothing more about it. Instead I said, "How's your shooting coming along?"

"It's coming back," Sly said. "I'll be ready to ride in a few more days."

"Well, by God," I said, "I'll be ready to ride with you."

"Good," he said. "Now, if you'll excuse me, I'll go get myself ready for lunch."

Now, I never did really understand all this gentleman kinda behavior. I never thought about getting ready for lunch. I always figgered if I was hungry, then I was ready, and the only thing to do was to find me some food and set down to eat it. But then, as you already know, I never was no gentleman. Sly was about halfway up the stairs when ole Happy looked up at me and said, "You mean to go after them Jaspers, then."

"Hell, yes," I said. "After what they done to me, I mean to kill their asses. Whichever ones Sly don't kill first."

"You sure you'll be up to it?" Happy asked me. "I mean, by the time Sly's ready to ride out, will you be all healed up and have your strength back and ever'thing?"

"I'll have enough of it back, Happy," I said. "It don't take a hell of a lot of strength to pull a trigger."

"Yeah, but a long ride like that can be real tiring," he said.

"Don't worry none about me," I said. "I'll manage it just fine."

About then ole Bonnie come on downstairs. She told

Aubrey to bring her some coffee, and she come right on over to set with me and Happy. "You feeling any better this morning, sweet'ums?" she said.

"I'm getting stronger with each day, honey pot," I said. "And I tell you what, darlin'. Before this day is over, I mean to take you back upstairs and show you just how much strength I done got back."

Chapter Fourteen

Well, after a while I went and showed her all right, but only I weren't near as good as what I thought I was going to be. Ole Bonnie, she tuck good keer of me, though, and she never made no complaints. I really got to hand it to her for that. Anyhow, I had just wore my ass out, and I went on back to sleep for a spell. Whenever I woke up, I thought about that. I didn't have no way of knowing just how soon ole Sly would be ready to hit the trail after them damned Jaspers, but I figgered I'd best not let him know how quick and easy I wore out or else he might not want to have me a-tagging along with him. I tuck me a little time a-waking up, and then I went on back down the stairs.

I tell you what, I never knowed before how a shooting-up like that could take it out of you, but I damn sure found out. You see, I hadn't never been all shot up like that before. I'd been stomped on pretty good, and as you know, I'd been throwed down the stairs, and I'd had my head busted a good many times, but I hadn't never been shot all to pieces like that. I figgered I was most nearly over the worst of it, though. I could get up and walk around, and I could even romp a bit with ole Bonnie, but I sure as hell did get tired quick and easy.

Back down in the bar, I had Aubrey fetch me my whiskey and tumbler, and I poured myself a good drink. Bonnie come and set with me. "Did you get all rested up, baby?" she asked me. "Aw, hell, yes, Bonnie," I told her. "I'm all right. I just got a little tired is all. You seen ole Sly in here?" She told me she hadn't saw him none, and then I recalled that ole Happy had told me that Sly was a-going out to practice his shooting, and so I figgered that's what he was likely up to.

Ole Peester come into the place just about then, and he come over to set with me and Bonnie. He tuck off his hat real polite-like and smiled, and I wondered what the slickery little bastard was up to. Then he said, "You seem to be coming along nicely, Barjack." I eyeballed him suspicious like, and I told him, "Yeah, I reckon I'm mending, all right." I thought about offering him a drink, but then I thought better of it, 'cause after all, selling drinks was my business, and I couldn't recall no time that I had gone into his office and he had offered me no free legal services. Aubrey come over and asked him if he wanted a drink, and he went and ordered hisself one, so it all worked out for the best. I made sure I seen him pay for it too. He tuck a little sissy sip.

"You know, Barjack," he said, "I've been thinking. It

might not be a bad thing at all to have Mister Sly living in our little town."

"Oh, yeah?" I said. "What the hell's changed your mind so drastic-like?"

"Well, after all," he said, "he's a well-known and highly respected shootist, and having him handy to call on in time of distress could be a real fine and handy thing. Why, he could help you out if something came up that you couldn't handle alone."

"I got Happy," I said.

"Yes," he said, "well, I meant, if something came up that you and Happy couldn't handle, just the two of you."

"Yeah," I said, "well, I s'pose you're right there, Mayor. Couldn't hurt nothing having him around."

"And if he's going to marry and settle down here," the damned ole mayor said, "why, I'm sure he'll develop a sense of civic responsibility and pride, and he'll find it in his interest to help maintain order here."

"I reckon he might just do that," I said.

"Uh, I understand that Mister Sly intends to go after the would-be assassins who shot him and you over at the county seat," Peester said, lowering his voice.

"Yeah," I said. "I seem to have heard a rumor to that effect my own self."

"How many of them are there?" Peester asked me.

"They's four of the sons of bitches left," I said.

"Could it be that you'll be going along with him?" he said.

"Could be," I said.

"So Mr. Bonapart will be left in charge here?" he said.

"He's the only depitty I got," I said. I lifted my glass

and tuck me a long drink. I was trying to figger out what ole Peester really had on his sneaky-ass little mind. Then I tuck me out a cigar and fired it up. Peester tuck hisself another little sissy sip.

"Well," Peester said, "I certainly wish you both a great deal of luck in your pursuit of those villains."

He left his drink, said good evening, and left on outa there. Bonnie looked at me with her face all kinda wrinkled up "What the hell was that all about?" she said.

"I ain't for sure," I said. "At first I kinda bought what he was saying. You know, that it would be a good thing to have ole Sly a-living here. But then I got to thinking. The little bastard ain't had no use for me for quite a spell now."

"But he's the one that hired you," Bonnie said.

"Hell, yeah," I said. "I know that. He hired me when this here was a mean-ass town, and I cleaned it up. Now I think he'd just as soon see me go. And you know, he never was comfterbul with ole Sly a-being here. No. I think he wanted to make sure that I was a-going with Sly and that we was a-going to be well outnumbered. He's hoping them Jaspers'll kill the both of us. That's what the hell he's a-hoping."

Sly come in then, and I waved him on over. He ordered hisself up a cup of coffee, and Aubrey brung it to him. "You been out a-shooting?" I asked him.

"Yes," he said. "I'm not quite up to snuff, but it's coming back. A few more days, and I think I'll be ready to ride. How about you, Barjack?"

"I'll be ready when you are," I said. "I'm real anxious to see those bastards again."

"Yes," Sly said. "As am I."

"You got any idea whichaway to go whenever we start in to hunting them?" I asked him.

"No," he said, "I don't. I figure we'll ride over to the county seat and ask around. See if anyone saw them leave town. It's not much, but we'll have to start somewhere."

"Yeah," I said. "Someone oughta have saw them ride out."

"Even so," Sly said, "once they got out of town, they could have turned in any direction. But I think the thing to do is check the nearest towns first. Even if they just rode through some place, someone there should know about it, and it will give us a direction. It may be slow at first, but we'll track them down."

"We damn sure will," I said. "If I could just only get myself a half a hour with that one they got over in the county jail, I bet your ass I could beat something outa him. He might know where the hell they mighta gone to."

"We could question him," Sly said. "He's not likely to tell us anything, but it wouldn't hurt to try it."

"I'd rather beat the crap out of him," I said, "or else stick a gun barrel in his mouth and halfway down his throat. I'd make him say something. I can promise you that."

Sly looked real thoughtful for a few seconds there, and then he said, "You know, Barjack, there just might be a way."

"A way to what?" I said.

"Oh," he said, "a way for me to distract the sheriff, maybe get him well away from his office and the jail, and give you the time to go in there and do—well, whatever it is you decide to do."

He grinned, and I grinned right back at him. It seemed like a damn good idea to me. Right after that, ole Sly excused hisself like the gentleman he was and went on upstairs. I wondered if he was a-needing his rest after being up so much of the day and being out a-practicing with his shooter and all. I kinda hoped that he was. I didn't really like thinking that he was so damn much tougher than me. Me and Bonnie set there a-talking and a-drinking, and I was still a-smoking my cigar. She was holding on to my arm the way she liked to do out in public, like as if she was a-showing the whole damn world that I belonged to her, and that was all right with me too. Pretty soon old Happy come in. He seen us and come over to set with us.

"You feeling all right, Barjack?" he said.

"Hell, yeah," I said. "I could rassle a goddamned grizzly bear right now." I was a-lying to him, of course. "What you doing in here in the middle of the day?"

"Why, it's suppertime, Barjack," he said. "I come to get me something to eat."

I guess I hadn't realized that it was so late in the day. I musta slept longer than what I thought. It come to me that I had oughta start in to keeping a better track of the time and just what the hell I was a-doing each day. I had me a big manhunt coming up, and the man I was a-going to be riding along with sure weren't no slouch. He was one of the best in the business. A real man-hunting son of a bitch. I didn't want him to be showing me up, and I damn sure didn't want to be a-slowing him down.

"Barjack," Happy said, "is it true that you and Sly are going after them Jaspers?"

"Hell," I said, "does ever'one in town know all of my damn business?"

"Well," Happy said, "it ain't a very big town. You know how things gets around."

"Yeah," I said, cutting him off. "We're going after the bastards."

"How you going to know where to look?" he asked me.

"We'll track their asses," I said. I didn't want to go repeating all the stuff me and ole Sly had said just a little while ago. I just weren't up to it.

"Track them, huh?" Happy said.

Aubrey come over and tuck Happy's supper order, and that made me feel like I was hungry too, so me and ole Bonnie, we each ordered us up a steak dinner too, and pretty soon the three of us was eating our supper there together. While we was in the middle of it, Sly come back downstairs. He was all dressed up real fine. He tipped his hat to us as he walked through headed for the front door, and I knowed he was a-going on over to the White Owl to let Miss Lillian fetch up his supper. Bonnie seen me a-looking after him, and the look she give me told me that she thought I was being jealous of ole Lillian, so I tried real hard to change the expression on my face, and just for good measure, I reached around her and give her a big hug, and then I give her a peck on the cheek, right there in front of ever'one in the whole damn place. I guess it worked, 'cause she never said nothing about me and Lillian.

Well, the days kept on a-going by, and I got a little

stronger each day and a little more anxious to get after them bastards what had shot me and ole Sly up so bad. I even had me a couple of good romps with ole Bonnie, 'bout as good as ever. Sly, he kept on a-shooting and getting hisself ready to go, and then final one day, it was a Wednesday, I think, ole Sly come around to me, and he said, "Do you feel ready to head out?" I said, "Hell, yes. When you want to go?" He said we'd ought to take a couple days to get our stuff together, and he was a-thinking that we'd head out early on Friday morning. I agreed, and I commenced to getting myself ready to go.

I had me a good horse what hadn't been doing nothing lately but eating and resting, and I figgered he'd be good for a long hard ride. Ole Sly, he had his own slick, black horse what he had come into town on. It was well rested and fed. I packed me a change of clothes. I didn't think I'd need no more than that, and I went over to my marshaling office and picked me out a good Winchester rifle and a shotgun, and I packed in plenty of ammunition for them two guns and for my ole Merwin and Hulbert Company revolver what I always wore.

I give ole Happy all kinds of instructions 'bout what to do and what not to do while I was gone, and I had Aubrey start in right away a-fixing and packing all kinds of food what would keep on the trail. I even picked up a couple extry canteens for hauling water. I meant to be well prepared for this here trip. There weren't no way of knowing how long we was going to be out a-looking for them Jaspers, and I didn't have no intention of having to abandon their trail 'cause I run out of supplies.

Me and ole Sly kept in touch concerning our readiness, and I told him not to worry about the food and water and such. I had the means of taking keer of that part, and he didn't need to do nothing along them lines. I made sure that Aubrey packed in the stuff I'd need for cooking along the way and a pot for making coffee, and then I had him stash me in a half-dozen bottles of my good booze. I knowed I would be a-needing that. Toward evening on Thursday, I tuck Sly into the back room at the Hooch House and showed him what all I had ready to go, and me and him agreed that we had ought to get us a packhorse to load ever'thing on. I told Aubrey to take keer of that little chore.

I'd got so busy that I hadn't noticed, but since I was a-fixing to ride out the next morning, I went to looking for ole Happy, and he weren't nowhere to be found. I even asked around about him, and I couldn't find no one what had saw him since Wednesday. I went down to the stable to check on his horse, and it was gone.

"Goddamn it," I said. "The weaselly little runt has gone and did it again. He's ran out on me in my hour of need. Next time I see that little son of a bitch, I'll just go on ahead and kill him. That's what I'll do." I went on out into the main big room and had Aubrey fetch me a drink, and just as I set down, here come ole Happy. He come right at me. I thought about pulling my revolver and just doing what I said, but I didn't want to kill him dead without him a-knowing how come I was doing it, so I waited for him to come on close, and I just stared hard at him and let him set down. He leaned on over towards me.

"They headed out southwest," he said.

"What?" I said.

"Them Jaspers," he said. "Whenever they left outa the

county seat, they headed southwest. I found that out, and then I sent a wire from the county seat down to Loganville, 'cause, you know, that's the first town they'd come into going in that direction, and the sheriff down there wired me back that, sure enough, they had rid through there. That's as far as I was able to track them thataway, but they headed southwest, and they went through Loganville. I just thought I'd try to save you a little time and travel if I could."

Well, I sure as hell felt guilty that I had been a-thinking about killing ole Happy for running out on me, and then come to find out that he hadn't never run out on me after all. The little bastard had went and rid over to the county seat and asked around and found out which way them Jaspers had gone right after they shot us up. And he had went even farther than that. He had went and sent that there wire and tracked their ass all the way to Loganville. Well, sure as hell, that was going to save me and ole Sly some time, 'cause the county seat was a few miles north of Asininity. We woulda rid up there, tuck some time in finding out what ole Happy had done found out for us, then we'd have had to head back southwest.

Well, I never said nothing about what all I was a-thinking. Instead I just shoved my bottle at ole Happy and said, "Have a drink on me, Happy." He knowed I was thanking him real special, 'cause I hardly ever bought him a drink. I made him pay his own bills there in the Hooch House. And I never give no one a drink outa my own special bottle. Well, almost never. His face kinda lit up there, whilst Aubrey fetched him over a glass. Yeah, he knowed how I felt about what he had did for me.

Later on in the evening, me and ole Bonnie went on upstairs to her room together, and we went and said our fond farewells for about half the night, and I found out for sure then that I was back up to snuff. I give her a hell of a good time, and she give the same and more right back to me. I thought again about how things was working out all around, and I knowed that ole Bonnie was the right and proper woman for me. I got to thinking about how I musta been crazy to get my ass hitched up with Lillian. I guess that I had just been kinda-like struck by lightning whenever I first seen her back then. Her being skinny like she was and all dressed up so fine and talking like a lady and ever'thing. She got to me, and I commenced to acting the fool over her. I'm just lucky that ole Bonnie didn't go on ahead and kill my ass back then. And now ever'thing was working out just fine and getting back to how it had used to be.

Then another thought come into my damn silly head. Here I was a-feeling so good about how things was working out so well in spite of all my previous foolishness, and I was a-fixing to light out first thing in the morning on the trail of four of the meanest sons of bitches what was loose out in that part of the country. Wouldn't it be stupid, I asked myself, just when things was a-looking so good, for me to ride out and get my ass blowed away for real? I thought about changing my mind about the whole deal and just letting ole Sly ride on after them Jaspers by his own self. He was a real professional killer. Likely he'd get all four of them bastards.

But when it come right down to it, I knowed that I couldn't do that. There was four of them and just one of him. If I let him go out by hisself, and they was to kill him, I wouldn't never forgive myself. And there was the fact that they had shot me up so bad. I wanted to kill at least some of them my own self, personal. I knowed it wouldn't never be enough to just only find out secondhand that someone else had kilt them. I had to have me a hand in it. Besides, I had faced as bad as them before and lived to tell about it.

Well, I tried to put all them kinds of thoughts outa my head and get back to concentrating on my sweet farewells to the massive flesh of my Bonnie, and I reckoned ole Sly had done said his proper and polite gentlemanly bye-byes to ole Lillian. I didn't nose into that none. Anyhow, after some more good romping and playing, me and ole Bonnie final went on to sleep.

Me and ole Sly met before sunup down in the main room of the Hooch House, and we commenced packing our one horse and saddling up the other two. I knowed I wouldn't see Bonnie again till it was all over and I come back to town. If I had dared to wake her up just only to say so long, hell, she'd likely sent me flying again. Lillian was up, though. Whenever we was final all mounted up and heading out of town, ole Sly excused hisself for a minute, and I watched him ride over to the house what had used to be my house, and there was ole Lillian a-standing on the front porch a-waiting. He rid over there and got down outa the saddle and give her a real fond embrace, and then he mounted up again and come on back over to join me. We headed on out.

"We don't need to ride north up to the county seat," I told him as we rid along kinda easy-like. Me and Sly was riding side by side, and I was a-leading the pack-horse. "Ole Happy went over there and done some checking for us. Them Jaspers rid outa there a-headed southwest, and they went through Loganville still a-headed that same direction."

"Well," Sly said, "in that case, we can ride straight down to Loganville and start our own tracking from there."

"That's what I figgered," I said.

"Your deputy saved us considerable time," he said. "I hope you thanked him properly for both of us."

"I done that all right," I said. 'Course, I knowed that what my kinda proper thanks and what Sly's kind was was two different things, but I never brung that up. "I thanked him real good and proper."

Chapter Fifteen

Me and Sly stopped somewheres around noon to rest up and fix us some vittles, and I weren't about to admit it out loud to him, but goddamn I was tired. I was damn near wore out from just that half a day's riding. I knowed it was on account of all them bullet holes I had just got over, or maybe I had ought to say, damn near got over. I remember wondering if he was a-feeling any the same way, but I figgered I'd never know, 'cause he was prob'ly like me. If he was a-tiring out sooner than what he used to, he wouldn't be saying nothing about it to me. That's for sure. Anyhow, we et us some beans and some jerky and hardtack, and we fixed us some coffee and drunk a few cups of that. Then we cleaned up our mess, and ole Sly says, "Are you about ready to ride, Barjack?"

"Sure," I said, really thinking that I'd just like to lay

still and rest up some more. But I never said nothing about that, of course, and so we packed up and mounted up and rid on out of there. I figgered we'd have us about a two-day ride on over to Loganville. Just mainly to make talk, I said, "Sly, when we catch up with them bastards, you got any kinda plan how we're going to go after them?"

"I haven't given it much thought," he said. "It will all depend on just where we find them. If they're in some town, it will have to be handled one way. If they're out on the trail, it will be a completely different situation. We'll just have to wait and see where we find them and take it from there."

Well, I figgered he was right about that, and I was sure a-hoping that we come across them out on the trail somewheres, 'cause thataway I could hunker down behind a big rock or something and blast away at them with my Winchester. I didn't know if ole Sly was aiming to face them fair and square or not, but I sure didn't have no intentions of doing nothing so damn foolish as that myself. Hell, if I was lucky enough to come up behind them, why, I figgered I'd just start in a-shooting the bastards in the back. After I had done shot the first one, or maybe two, well, likely the other'ns would get turned around and try to shoot back, but I figgered I'd sure as hell start out thataway, backshooting the sons of bitches.

We was maybe halfway into the afternoon when we run into our first trouble. We was riding along the trail there a-minding our own business when a goddamned rattler spooked our horses. Mine rared on up real quick-like and surprising. I weren't expecting it, and he spilled me off his back end. Goddamn, that landing hurt. Sly's mount started in to skittering, which caused him to be some slow on the draw, but the worst of it was that our packhorse fell over and broke his damn leg.

Soon as Sly got control of his horse, he whipped that Colt out like lightning and shot the head right offa that snake. I never seen nothing like it. Fast and accurate. Both. Then he turned right to me and said, "Are you all right, Barjack?"

I pulled my ass up offa the ground real slow and easy and straightened myself up, groaning the whole time— and for good reason, too. "Yeah," I said. "I think so. But that damn packhorse don't look so good." Sly put the poor son of a bitch outa his misery, and we went to unpacking ever'thing and repacking it onto the back ends of our two saddle horses. It was all we could do. Then we went to riding again.

We didn't talk too much. I reckon we both knowed what it was we was up to, and there weren't no reason to be a-talking about it, and that was about the only thing on our minds, so we just rid along side by side and quiet-like. We rid the day away like that, and then we made us a camp for the night. We et, and I hauled out one of my whiskey bottles. I tuck me a nice long drink, and I offered one to Sly, but he turned it down.

Well, he was asleep before me, so I just kept on a-drinking, and I got to wondering what the hell was going on back in ole Asininity. I wondered if ole Bonnie was taking any cowhands up to her room while I was outa town. I didn't like to think that while I was a-sleeping on the ground in the cold, she might be back there a-bouncing someone in her bed. I wondered if Happy was holding things together, too. Fin'ly I drunk me enough whiskey that I put all them kinda thoughts outa my head and went on to sleep.

Whenever I woke up in the morning, ole Sly done had the coffee made. I fixed us up some breakfast, and we et. Then we cleaned up our campsite, packed and saddled our horses, and lit out again. I figgered we'd make Loganville by that night—if we was to ride long enough. If it was to get dark on us before we made it, we'd likely have to spend one more night on the trail and then get into the place early the next day.

Well, nothing much happened that day, nothing to talk about anyhow, and I was right about our timing. The sun was a-getting low in the sky, and there still weren't no sign of life up ahead of us, so we camped out again. We et us another supper on the trail and slept another night on the ground by a campfire. I drunk some more whiskey that night and slept the rest of the night good and hard. The next morning, we had us a trail breakfast, cleaned up, packed and saddled up, and headed on. We come to Loganville about midmorning.

It weren't much of a town. Hell, it weren't even as big as Asininity. It didn't have no hotel, just a small what you might call rooming house. There was a place where you could buy a meal or a drink, and there was a general store, then a few scattered houses. They did have a sheriff's office with just only one jail cell, and they had a telegraph. That was just about it. Me and Sly went straight to the sheriff's office, hitched our mounts, and went inside. The sheriff we found in there was paunchier than me, and I think he was older, too. When we walked in, he looked up from behind his desk and said, "Howdy, strangers. What can I do for you?"

I jumped in right quick, on accounta I weren't at all sure what ole Sly would say if I didn't. It didn't seem like the smartest thing in the world to go into a new town and announce first thing that he was the famous and infamous Widdermaker. "I'm Barjack," I said, "town marshal over to Asininity."

"Oh, yeah," he said, "I've heard of you. I'm Sheriff Johnny Hoig. What brings you to Loganville?"

We shuck hands, and then Hoig reached out to shake hands with Sly, and I jumped in again. I didn't want ole Sly to even mention his name. "Me and my partner here," I said, "we're tracking four hardcase outlaws name of Jasper."

"You're kind of out of your jurisdiction, ain't you?" Hoig said.

"Yeah," I said. "That's right, and I know it, but them Jaspers shot the two of us up pretty bad a while back, and we aim to get the bastards. I ain't acting in my official capacity. You might say me and my partner here is acting like bounty hunters, or maybe just private citizens out to settle a grudge. The main thing is we're after them, and we mean to get them. I heard they come through here."

"They did that, all right," said Hoig. "It's been a while back now. I'm pleased to say they didn't cause no real trouble while they was here, but they was acting kind of rowdy, and I was sure relieved when they finally left."

"Do you know which way they were going when they left town?" Sly asked.

"I know more than that," Hoig said. "I heard them say they were headed for New Mexico."

Well, we went on over to the one place in town where you could buy a meal, and we got us a steak and taters what someone else cooked. It weren't the best I ever had, but it was better than what we'd been eating on the trail. I was thinking about New Mexico. I sure hoped we wouldn't have to chase them that damn far, but at least we knowed their general direction of travel. The other thing was that if they was headed south and southwest like that, at least it would be a-getting warmer all along the way. We was about halfway through our meal whenever ole Sly spoke up.

"You avoided mentioning my name to that sheriff very cleverly," he said.

"Yeah," I said. "Well, I weren't at all sure that it would be the best thing for him to know just who the hell you are."

"I suspect you're right about that," he said.

We finished up our food and ordered up another refill on our coffee, and then I said to Sly, "What do you think? We got us a half a day left. Do we ride it on out or stop here for the night?"

"If we ride," he said, "we close the gap that much more. On the other hand, it would feel good to sleep in a bed. You know, since the shooting, I tire out much more quickly than I used to."

Goddamn but I was glad to hear him say that. I weren't the only one. I decided to admit the truth to him too then, since he had done admitted it to me. "Yeah," I said. "Me too." We went on over to the rooming house and got us a room. They had plenty of beds. Loganville weren't the busiest little town I had ever stopped over in. Well, we still had us an afternoon to waste, and I

187

was tired, but I weren't sleepy, so I decided to spend the rest of the day right there in that little eating and drinking place. I ordered me up a whiskey, and it weren't too bad. Sly, he stuck by me, but he drunk coffee. It musta been nigh onto five o'clock whenever ole Hoig come in there and found us. He come right over to our table.

"I just got a wire," he said. "You'll be interested."

"What is it?" I said.

"Them Jaspers," he said. "They stopped over in Dog Creek, south of here."

"I know the place," I said.

"They killed a man, then lit out," Hoig said. "Still headed south or southwest. They sent out a posse after them, but it come back empty-handed. Thought you'd like to know."

"When did all this happen?" Sly asked.

"Just last night," Hoig said.

"That means they're about four days ahead of us," I said. Then, looking up at ole Hoig, I added, "That about right?"

"Yeah," he said "About four days, I'd say."

"And with a posse on their ass," I said, "they was likely moving fast outa Dog Creek."

"Yeah," Sly said, kinda musing-like.

"What say we hit the sack early then and get us a good early start in the morning," I said. "We might oughta move fast for a while to catch up some. Then slow down again later on down the trail."

"That's a good idea, Barjack," Sly said. "A couple of good ideas."

We thanked ole Hoig for the information and went on over to the rooming house. I tuck a bottle with me in case I couldn't get right to sleep, but as it turned out, I didn't really have no trouble. Damn, I thought, but this here traveling is wearing my ole ass out. I knowed it was the bullet holes that was the cause of it, though, and I went to sleep a-cussing the goddamn Jaspers.

It was a long stretch from Loganville to Dog Creek, and it was boring as hell, but it did get a little warmer the farther we moved south. We rid along fast for a while, then slowed down so we wouldn't ruin our horses. We done like that for a couple of days. Then we moved along more or less normal for the next two days. There ain't nothing much more to say about the rest of that part of the trip. We come into Dog Creek kinda late, so we just got us some beds for the night, figgering to ask our questions in the morning. I was tired as hell and went right to sleep after only a couple of good snorts of booze.

The next morning after we'd had us a greasy breakfast at a local eating place follered by a few cups of coffee what tasted like lamp oil, me and ole Sly went and looked up the local law, which in Dog Creek they called a constable. The feller's name was Hack Thurmond. We told him we was on the trail of them Jaspers what had did a killing in his town, and we asked him if his posse had did any good.

"They come back empty," Thurmond told us. "Tracked them a good ways southwest and had to give it up."

I give Sly a look and said, "It seems like as if they ain't changed their plans none."

"What plans is that?" Thurmond said.

189

"Aw, we just heard that the bastards was headed for New Mexico," I said. "That's all."

"Well, fellers," Thurmond said, "if you catch up with them and live through it, I hope you'll stop back by and let me know."

"We'll do that," I said.

"That's a promise," Sly added.

We packed up and headed our asses southwest. I had thought that the weather would keep getting warmer the souther we went, but it was only about midafternoon whenever it commenced to snowing. We kept on a-going, but it become obvious in just a while that it weren't a-fixing to let up no time soon. In fact, the snow kept a-getting heavier and the damn snowflakes bigger.

"Damn it, Sly," I said, "we're going to have to hole up somewheres. We can't keep going in this."

"I'm afraid you're right," he said. "What do you suggest?"

We had been riding along the edge of a pretty big ranch for some miles, so I said, "Let's see if we don't come across a line shack somewheres soon. If we don't, we're just going to have to stop and make do with a camp. Try to find some trees and throw together some kinda shelter."

Well, we never found no line shack, but we did come across some trees alongside a creek in another few miles, and we decided we had better stop there if we knowed what the hell was good for us. We rid on into the trees, tuck keer of our horses, and started in to making camp. It was a good thing we had packed in so many provisions, too. We used us a couple of extra blankets to fashion out a kinda lean-to shelter there under them trees, and we fixed up our sleeping space on down underneath there. We also built us up a fire for cooking over and for keeping us a little warmer under the edge of that shelter. I fetched us some fresh water from the creek, and we had us a pot of coffee going pretty damn quick. It was still a bit early for our next meal.

"Goddamn it," I said, as we was waiting for the coffee to boil on up, "this here snow is going to slow us up somewhat, and it will damn sure wipe out any tracks them Jaspers has left behind."

"It could be worse than that," he said. "If it's not snowing on south where they are, they'll be able to get even farther ahead of us than they are already."

"Damn it," I said.

"There's no use worrying about it," Sly said. "It's already on us. The best we can do is deal with it. At least we know what direction they're heading, and if their pattern holds, it's not difficult to trace their movements. Every place they go through they leave an impression."

"That's for sure," I said.

It kept on a-snowing all that afternoon, and we fin'ly cooked us our evening meal and et it. I left off the coffee then and pulled out one of my bottles. Ole Sly still wouldn't drink no whiskey. It become obvious to me that he meant to stay cold sober at least till our little job was did. But me, I finished off that bottle that evening. When it come dark the snow was still a-falling, and we crawled on under our covers for the night. I slept like a damn log, but Sly musta got up ever' now and then during the night, 'cause our fire was still a-going good whenever I woke up the next morning. It had quit snowing, but the snow was deep all around us. We made some coffee and some breakfast, and we et.

"We ain't going to move very fast in that pile of white," I said.

"No, we're not," Sly said. "But it looks to me like it's over, and the sun's coming out strong. I think we won't have to wait it out too much longer."

So we done that, and sure enough, that ole sun come out and commenced to melting the snow. There was already enough piled up, though, that it weren't going to melt it down right away. By midafternoon, we figgered we'd be able to ride out the next morning. "That'll put them bastards at least five days ahead of us," I said.

"When they get far enough south to feel safe," Sly said, "they'll stop to rest and play somewhere. We'll catch up with them."

We spent one more night in that place, and then we headed out. The snow weren't too deep no more, but in places it was sure as hell muddy. But the sun stayed out good and warmed the air up enough to make it at least tolerable. I was glad for that. We rid on for another day and come to a little town. It sure weren't nothing to brag on, and if it had a name I never seen it nowhere and never heard it called. We couldn't find no law, and so we asked in the saloon if them Jaspers had been through.

"Four men that fits your description rode through here about five days ago," the barkeep said. "They stopped in here and had a couple drinks, then went on."

They hadn't caused no trouble, so he didn't have nothing more to say about them, but at least we knowed we was still on the right trail. I had me one drink in there just kinda to show my appreciation for the information, and then me and Sly went on our way. For two days nothing more happened to talk about. We was in open country, and the weather was better. Neither me nor Sly knowed just exactly where we was at, and we slept and et at campsites along the way. Then we come onto a place called North Dooley. It was a fair size. We was both of us wore out from all of our traveling, so we hunted up a place to stay. It was a real actual hotel with a eating place and a saloon downstairs. We got us rooms, unpacked for the night, stabled our horses, and ordered us up a real good meal. Sly went on up to bed, but I went into the saloon for a drink or two.

Then I seen them. All four of them. I had only saw the bastards that one time, and not for very long neither, 'cause they started into blasting me just as I got my look at them. But I knowed them nonetheless. It was the Jaspers, all right. I tell you, I swallered hard. I was ready for them all four to start in to shooting again, but they never. They never even hardly looked at me, so I fin'ly figgered that they had been so intent on blasting ole Sly's ass away, they hadn't even tuck theirselves a good look at me. I finished my drink and left that saloon and went straight up to our room. Sly was sleeping, but I woke his ass up, and he come awake with his gun in his hand. When he seen it was just only me, he lowered it on down.

"What is it, Barjack?" he said.

"They're right down there in the saloon," I said. "All four of them. I seen them just bigger'n life. I guess they never recognized me, but I knowed them, all right."

"The Jaspers?" he said. "They're here?"

"Like you said," I went on, "they must feel safe. They

193

musta stopped to rest and play right here. We've done caught up with the bastards, Sly. Now, what the hell're we going to do?"

Well, he was wide awake then, and he was a-setting up on the bed. He didn't answer me right away. He set there a-thinking real hard. Then he said, "We're going to kill them, but we have to decide how and where and when."

Chapter Sixteen

Well, ole Sly, he said we couldn't just go out there a-blasting away at them bastards on account of someone innocent down there might get in the way of some bullets, and we sure as hell didn't want that a-happening. We'd have to catch them out in the open somehow, like out in the street whenever there wasn't no one else in the way, or else outside of town. I reckoned as how I could get my rifle and just start in to picking them off right then and there from up at the top of the stairs before any of them knowed what the hell was going on, but he nixed that idee, good as it was. They might start in to shooting back before I was to get all four of them, he said, and the law would most for sure get involved, too. We didn't want that. Besides all that, he said, he just didn't work thataway. He always give the other feller a chance.

"Hell, I don't," I said. "Matter a fact, I try my damndest not to give him no chance at all."

"We're not doing it that way, Barjack," he said.

"Well, what the hell do we do, then?" I said. "Just wait around here for all four of them to take a Sunday ride outa town? If we do that, hell, they just might hang around here for a good long spell, and you can't leave the damn room for fear they see you. They know you, all right. It was you they was a-trying to kill whenever they shot us up the way they done. If you go down outa this room, and one of them Jaspers is to get a look at you, why hell, he'll start in a-shooting all right, and they won't be worrying about no innocent get-in-the-ways."

"That's true enough," he said. "Even so, let's wait awhile and see what we can find out about their plans."

I reckoned he meant for me to see what I could find out, on account of him having to stay hid out in the room, but I didn't make no argument with him. Goddamn, I wanted to start in blasting their asses. We had been out on a long trail after the sons of bitches, and damn it, they was right there. I jammed my hat down on my head and stalked toward the door.

"Barjack," Sly said, "where are you going?"

"Don't worry," I said. "I ain't going to start nothing."

I went back downstairs and got me a bottle and a glass and set my ass down right near them Jaspers where I could hear most ever' word they said, and then I commenced to drinking whiskey like as if there weren't never going to be no more of the stuff. Now you know enough about me by now that you know I can drink a hell of a lot of whiskey and still know pretty well what's going on around me, but I figgered if I was to drink enough and be obvious about my drinking, why, any stranger would think that I was drunker'n a skunk. So that there was my plan. After a while, I just dropped my ole head down on the table with a good loud thunk like as if I had done passed out. It worked. I heard one of them bastard Jaspers laugh at me.

"Son of a bitch can't hold his liquor," he said.

"Look at that bottle," another'n said. "He drank a hell of a lot in a short time. No wonder he's passed out already."

"A real drunk," said another'n.

Then I guess they just kinda forgot about me, and they went on a-talking about this and that. But my playacting and the little bump I give myself on the noggin paid off eventual. I heard one of them four say in a low voice, "What are we going to do about that stagecoach?" Then another'n said, "Just keep quiet about it. We know it's coming, and we know what it's carrying. What we don't know, 'cause we ain't familiar with this country down here, we don't know where will be a good place to stop it. First thing in the morning, I'm going out and ride that road and figger that one out."

"We'll go with you," one of them said.

"No you won't," said the first'n. "If you three stick here in town and make sure folks sees you around, they might not even notice that I'm gone. In fact, I'd say that you'd oughta split up at least once or twice and let someone see just one of you somewheres around town. They might think they're still seeing all of us if they see you one at a time here and there around town. When I got it all figgered out, I'll come back. Then we'll ride out in time to get the job done."

"Well, all right," one of them said.

"Drink up," said the bossy one. "Let's get the hell outa here. I mean to be up and outa here early."

I listened while they scooted their chairs back and then tromped on outa the place, and then I rolled my head real slow just in case, and I opened one eye, and when I seen that they was really and for sure gone, I got up and went over to the door to take a look, and I seen the four of them walk into a hotel across the way. Then I went on back upstairs to tell ole Sly what all I had learnt.

"We can get one of them out all by his lonesome," I said.

"That's good, Barjack," he said. "What we don't know is just how early he means to ride out in the morning."

"I s'pose we could spell each other setting at the winder and watching the hotel over yonder," I said.

"All right," he said. "We'll do that."

It musta been around five in the morning whenever I seen that Jasper come out the front door of the hotel across the street. He pulled down his hat and ducked his head against the cold night air and headed for the stable. I shuck Sly awake, and he come over to the winder to look.

"Let's get ready to go," he said.

I was already dressed, but I pulled on my heavy coat and strapped on my six-gun. Then I got my hat and my Winchester and my shotgun. Sly had to get hisself all the way dressed, so 'stead of waiting on him there in the room, I went on out. I kinda lurked in the dark out

198

there on the main street, and I watched to see which way outa town ole Jasper tuck out whenever he come outa that there stable. He rid out going west. Pretty quick after that, here come Sly. We hustled on down to the stable and saddled our own horses, and I told him the direction Jasper had rid. We went after him. I got in kinda a hurry, but Sly slowed me down.

"We can't see him up there in the dark," he said. "We don't want to ride up on him until we're ready."

"But what if he turns off somewheres?" I said.

"You said he's checking a stage route," Sly said. "He'll have to stay on the main road."

I reckoned ole Sly had to be right about that one, so I slowed my ass on down and kept my mouth shut. It was nippy cold, though, and I was anxious to get the job did and get on back to town. Well, we moseyed along like that till the sun showed itself, and I was sure glad to see that. It would take it a little while, but it would give us some light, and it would warm the air up at least some little bit. I weren't paying too much attention, I guess, 'cause Sly surprised me whenever he reached over and put a hand on my chest to stop me. I whoaed my horse, and me and Sly stopped side by side there in the road. He pointed up ahead, and I squinnied up my eyes some to get me a good look. There was that Jasper, all right. He was still a fair distance ahead of us and just riding along easy-like.

"He don't know we're on his trail," I said.

"No," said Sly. "You see where the road starts to drop down up there?"

I told him I did. The ground on either side of the road, just about where ole Jasper was a-riding, begun to rise, and the road went down like as if it was going down into a valley or something.

"Let's get off the road," Sly said, "and try to ride up above him and around ahead of him."

So we done that. We rid a good ways offa the road on the left or south side, and we got far enough off that we felt like we could ride a little harder and faster, and he wouldn't hear our horses pounding by him whenever we got on up that far. We moved out at a pretty good clip then, and on down the trail, we slowed down again. Both of us figgered that we was likely well out ahead of Jasper. We stopped, and Sly dismounted and walked on over to the road. Pretty soon he come back.

"We're ahead of him, all right," he said, "but not far. He's still moving slow. Let's get a little farther ahead and then prepare to meet him."

We rid on some more, and then we turned and rid on down to the road. Sly spotted a place where the road curved, and we went down there. He rid right out in the middle of the road where ole Jasper would come a-riding around the curve and all of a sudden see him there. Then he picked out me a spot offa the road.

"Go right over there, Barjack," he said. "He won't be able to see you, but I will. When you see him about to come around this curve, wave your hat at me. But don't do anything else. If he kills me, then you can take it your way from there."

What he meant by that was that if Jasper was to outshoot him, then I could go on ahead and shoot Jasper in the back with my Winchester if I was a mind to. I never thought there was much chance of things working out thataway, but I went on and got myself ready just the same. I went on over to my spot, and I tuck out my Winchester and made sure it was ready to fire, and then I watched for that Jasper. Whenever you're a-waiting like that, it seems like as if a thing takes forever, but really it couldn'ta been but only a few minutes. Here he come. I waited till he was just ready to make that there curve, and I pulled off my hat and waved it. Then I watched.

Jasper rid around that curve, and he was sure surprised, all right. He jerked his horse to a stop, and then he set there and didn't move.

"Hello, Jasper," Sly said.

"I thought we killed you," Jasper said.

"You failed," said Sly, "but I mean to kill you right here and now."

"Well, now, wait a minute, Sly," Jasper said. "Can't we talk this over?"

"No," Sly said. "There's nothing to talk about."

"Ain't it true what they say about you, then?" Jasper said. "About you never going for your gun first?"

"I guess you'll go for your gun, all right," said Sly. "If you don't go first, you have no chance of beating me."

"But if you won't go first," Jasper said, "and I don't go, then you can't shoot me."

Sly pulled out his Colt and pointed it at Jasper. Then he clumb down outa the saddle. He told Jasper to do the same, and he done it.

"I still ain't going to draw on you," Jasper said. Sly holstered his Colt and walked right up close to Jasper. Then he slapped him across the face. Jasper staggered back, and Sly stepped after him and slapped him again.

"Damn you," Jasper yowled, and Sly slapped him real hard. Ole Jasper, he turned his back on Sly to keep Sly from slapping his face, and Sly just grabbed the hat right offa Jasper's head and commenced to beating him across the head and back and shoulders with it. "Stop it," Jasper hollered. He had his face huddled in his arms. "Stop it, damn you." Of a sudden, ole Sly lifted up his right foot and put the sole of his boot right on ole Jasper's ass, and then he pushed good and hard, and Jasper, he went flying forward and fell on his face.

Well, sure enough, he rolled over and come up with a six-gun in his hand, but it weren't even up and leveled before the blast from Sly's Colt roared out and echoed through that valley. Jasper's hand just went limp. His shooter dangled there on his trigger finger for a couple of seconds, and his head slumped forward. Then he laid on back, and he never moved no more. God a'mighty damn. I ain't never saw such a fast shot as what I had saw just then. I realized that I was a-holding my breath, and I let it out and then sucked in some new air.

"Goddamn, Sly," I said, walking on down into the road to join him there. "I ain't never saw nothing like that."

He was a-reloading that Colt's empty chamber what he had just emptied right into that ole Jasper's heart. I come on up beside him. "I've been practicing," he said.

"What're we a-going to do about this one here?" I said.

"I'll drag him off the road," Sly said, "and roll him in the ditch. Someone might notice him one of these days."

"I'll just go and fetch my horse," I said.

Whenever I come back all mounted up, ole Sly had done rolled Jasper into the ditch beside the road. He was climbing on board his own mount. I rid up beside him there. I had damn near forgot all about feeling tired and cold. I was all excited, and I wanted to go get them others. "Just three left," I said.

"Yeah," he said.

I reached down into my saddlebag and come out with a bottle. I uncorked that son of a bitch and had me a long pull on it. Damn but it was good out there in the early-morning cold like that. I offered it over to ole Sly, but he waved it away.

"No, thanks," he said.

I tuck me a good look at ole Sly just then, and he sure did look to be serious and somber. Me, I was feeling good. Hell, if I'da been the one what had just shot and kilt me one of them Jasper bastards, I'da been dancing me a jig. He sure was a funny one, that Widdermaking son of a bitch. I tuck another drink and put my bottle away.

"All right, then," I said. "What now?"

"We go back to town," he said, "and wait. Sooner or later, the others will wonder why this one hasn't come back. They'll make some kind of move then. We'll take it from there."

"How we going to get your ass back into the hotel without them a-seeing you in the daylight?" I asked him.

"We'll ride in easy," he said. "As long as they're not out in the street, I ought to be able to ride around to the back of the hotel and slip in."

Well, the ride back was slow and cold, what with the excitement all behind us for the time being, but eventual we made it on back to town, and we done it the way he had said. We went in slow, and we didn't see them Jaspers. We went around behind the hotel, and Sly got offa his horse and went into the back door. I got offa mine and went to stand just inside the door to make sure no Jaspers was in there a-looking. They wasn't, and he made it to the stairs all right.

I went back out then and tuck both horses back down to the stable and unsaddled and unpacked them and put them away. I told that liveryman there to give them a good rub and to feed them some oats, and he promised me he'd do that. Then I walked on back to the hotel and went on up to the room. Up in the room I found Sly a-standing at the winder looking out over the main street.

"See anything?" I asked him.

"No Jaspers," he said.

"I didn't see none of them either," I said. "Say, you hungry? You need me to fetch you anything up here?"

"I hate to treat you like a manservant, Barjack," he said, "but I could use a breakfast and some coffee."

"It ain't no trouble," I said. I left the room and went downstairs and ordered up double what ole Sly wanted, and while I was a-waiting for it, I had myself a drink. Before the food was ready, I had to have another. Final, the barkeep brung me out a platter. He looked at all them eggs and steak and bread and the pot of coffee there, and he told me how much, and I paid him. Then he said, "You must be awful hungry."

"I always eat me a good breakfast," I said. "It starts the day out right."

Back up in the room, I put down the tray and went into my trail stuff what I had packed along and fetched me out a fork and a tin cup. I couldn'ta asked for double that stuff without making someone suspicious that I was a-feeding two of us up there. Me and ole Sly both et like we was nigh about to starve, and we finished off that whole pot of coffee, too. He thanked me like the gentleman he was, and I put the dirty dishes, all except my own personal ones, back onto the tray and stuck the tray on the floor outside of the room.

"You reckon that'll hold you till lunchtime?" I asked him.

"I think so," he said. "Thanks, Barjack."

"Ah, hell," I said. "Nothing to it. Listen here, I think I'll go on back down and nose around some."

I found the three remaining Jaspers in another bar, and they was already drinking that early in the day. I weren't the only one. The bar weren't none too crowded, so I didn't see no way to plant myself too close to them without causing them to suspicion me, so I just bellied up to the bar and ordered me a whiskey. They didn't have my favorite brand, and it weren't none too good, but it was whiskey all right, so I drank it on down. I made a face and a noise and shoved that glass away from myself. "Rotgut mule piss," I said. I heard someone laugh behind me, and I turned around to look. It was them Jaspers.

"You're right about that, pard," one of them said. "I was just thinking the same thing." Then he turned to his brothers and added, "Let's go on back over to that other place. They got better booze." They all got up and throwed some money on the table and started out, but then the one what had spoke to me looked back at me. "Come on along with us," he said. Well, by God, I did.

205

. We wound up back over at the same place where me and ole Sly was staying right upstairs, and we ordered up a good bottle of whiskey and all of us set down at a table together. I felt some strange a-doing that, but I reckon it proved once and for all that them bastards never recognized me at all. They had shot me to pieces and damn near kilt me, and all for nothing. I was just standing too close to ole Sly was all. I figgered they was the worst kind of killing sons of bitches there was. Why, hell, it coulda been a woman or a kid a-standing there.

Anyhow, we got us drinks poured all around, and that one what liked to talk, he raised his glass up like for a toast. "Here's to good, hard drinking men," he said. I said, "I'll drink to that," and we all turned up our glasses. "What's your name?" that ole boy said to me then, and I felt a couple seconds of panic, 'cause even though they never recognized me, they still mighta knowed my name. I come out with the first thing that popped into my thick skull, and it was ole Happy's last name.

"Bonapart," I said.

That one laughed. The others never. "Like in Napoleon?" he said.

"Yeah," I said. "Just like that." I wondered if them other two knowed who the hell Napoleon was, but I never asked them. I just poured myself another drink.

"Well, Napoleon," that Jasper said, "I seen you drinking in here last night, and I seen that you drank a hell of a lot of whiskey before you went and passed out. I'm Orvel Jasper, and these here are my brothers. This is Orren, and this here is Bud."

"Howdy, boys," I said.

"I like your style, Napoleon," Orvel said, "and I think we'll just all get as drunk as hell together here today."

Chapter Seventeen

Well, hell, we commenced to working on that very task, but the only thing was, I was making out to be just as drunk as them others, but I weren't, not by a long shot. I never met a man who can hold as much liquor as me, but I let them Jaspers think that maybe they could. Whenever their speech started in to getting fuzzy, why, I went and let mine do the same thing, and whenever they started into staggering a little bit when they stood up to take a few steps, hell, I got rubbery legged too. But only, I weren't for real. It was all a act I was a-putting on for their benefit.

It was a-getting along about toward evening, and we'd had us a few hours of drinking. I seen that ole Bud was just almost did in from it. The other two was staggering and talking mushy, but they seemed like as if they would be able to go on for a while yet. We had just emptied a bottle and ordered up a fresh one. Orvel, he leaned in real close to me and said, "Napoleon, I'm going to tell you something." The bartender come over with the bottle, and Orvel set back again and shut up. Whenever the barkeep walked away, Orvel leaned on back in towards me. "I'm fixing to tell you something," he said, "but you can't tell no one else, not a living son of a bitch."

I kinda weaved around some in my chair like as if I couldn't hardly set straight no more. "All right," I said. "I can keep a secret as good as the next bastard."

"Well, listen to this here, Napoleon," Orvel said. "Me and my brothers here, we got us another brother. There's four of us altogether. Used to be eight, but that widow-making son of a bitch Herman Sly killed poor ole Ormond. We got Sly for it, though. Blasted his ass real good, but only, we lost three more in the doing of it. So anyhow, there's just the four of us now, and our brother Oliver is out right now a-looking over a . . . situation."

"Hey, Orvel," Orren said, "you hadn't oughta be talking about that."

"Oh, hell," Orvel said, "Napoleon here is all right. I'm fixing to ask him to throw in with us on this deal. You know, we are some shorthanded now."

Bud was a-hanging his head like as if he was just about ready to pass on out anytime, and ole Orren, after he had put in his two or three cents' worth to the conversation and then got answered back short, why, he just kinda flopped back in his chair like he didn't have no more arguing left in him nowhere. Orvel leaned in even closer to me.

"I like you, Napoleon," he said. "Here's the deal. Ole Oliver is out scouting the road where the stagecoach is going to come over it on its way to here in just a few days. You see, we got us word that it's a-going to be carrying a special strongbox full of cash for the bank here. Well, we mean to see that cash box don't make it all the way through. We mean to stop it and take that cash for ourselves—and you, if you'll throw in with us."

"Well, hell," I said in my slurriest speech, "how come you to want to be so nice to me like that? You don't hardly even know me."

"I know you good enough," he said. "And I like you. I done told you that. Well? What do you say?"

"When's this going to happen?" I asked him.

"Day after tomorrow," Orvel said. "Afternoon."

"Well, by God," I said, "I ain't got nothing else going, and I ain't got enough money in my britches to last me much longer, neither. I say, why the hell not?"

"Good," Orvel said, and he slapped me on the back and leaned back in his chair to relax.

"Orvel," I said, "I don't reckon in my whole entire life anyone has done anything near so nice as this what you just done for me. I just don't hardly know what the hell to say to you."

"Well, shit," he said, "don't get all blubbery on me."

Well, I kinda slobbered a little bit and wiped my eyes and my mouth with my sleeve, and then I tuck myself another drink. Both a them other Jaspers had done passed clean out with their heads on the table. Orvel was the toughest, and I figgered I had to stay ahead of him but not let on to him that I was. I wanted to get away and let ole Sly know just what it was I had fell into.

"Your brothers has give up on us," I said.

"Yeah," he said. "They do that. It's kinda embarrassing for me, but, hell, they're my brothers. I better lug them on over to our room, though, while I can still walk."

"I'll help you," I said.

Me and ole Orvel both stood up on wobbly legs, and each one of us hauled a Jasper brother up onto our shoulders. Then we went to staggering out through the front door and on across the street. Right smack out in the middle of the street, ole Orvel fell down and him and his brother both went sprawling. I put down my load and helped him get back up and load up again, and then I got mine back up onto my own shoulder, and we made it the rest of the way into the hotel across the street where they had a room. We got them into the room and tossed them onto a bed. They was two beds in there, and we tossed them both on just one. I headed for the door.

"Where you going, Napoleon?" Orvel asked me.

"Hell," I said, "we left some whiskey in that bottle. Let's go finish it off."

Orvel had dropped his ass into a chair, so he started to get up, but his ole legs just wouldn't rise him up from that chair. He dropped back down real heavy. Then he kinda waved at me. "Ah, hell," he said, "you go on and finish it up for me. I can't make it. I'll see you tomorrow."

I slurred him a good night and went staggering outa the room, but just as soon as I got out, I straightened my ass up and moved right along. I got back across the street, picked up the bottle we had left on the table there, along with my glass, and hurried right upstairs to find ole Sly. He was a-setting at a small table with a deck of cards all spread out and playing hisself a game of solitaire. I reckoned life in that room like he was a-living must be awful boring and a whole hell of a lot like being in jail. He looked up and said, "Hello, Barjack."

"Howdy," I said. "You need anything before I go on ahead and sack out?"

"I am hungry," he said.

"I'll fetch you up something," I said. I was feeling real smug a-holding back the good news like that. I went back down and ordered up a couple of steak dinners, and that barkeep give me another one of them funny looks. I said, "Hell, I didn't eat no lunch." I had me a little drink of whiskey while I was a-waiting, and in a little while he brung them out, and I paid for them. I tuck them and hurried back up to the room. Me and ole Sly went to work on them without saying much. I washed mine down with whiskey. He drunk water. When we was both done, I decided to tell him the news.

"I got drunk with them Jasper boys," I said.

He looked up right smart. "You did?" he said.

"I sure as hell did," I said. "And I outdrunk them, all three. I left them passed out in their room across the street."

"Goddamn," he said, and it was the first time I ever did hear ole Sly say anything even a little bitty bit off color, as they say. "You might be able to get us some good information that way."

"I done already did that," I said, and I just set back and grinned like a ole dog what's been rolling in fresh cow dung.

"All right, Barjack," Sly said, "don't make me drag it out of you."

"Okay, then," I said, "here it is. That one what you

killed? He was out scouting up a good spot to rob the stage from. Stage is a-coming into town day after tomorry with some cash on it, so they heard. They're planning to rob it out there. 'Course, they don't know yet that their brother's out there dead alongside the road."

"That bit of news might change their plans, and it might not," he said. "Day after tomorrow, huh?"

"In the afternoon," I said. "And there's more."

"Tell me," he said, "before I wring your neck."

"They done asked me to throw in with them on the deal," I told him. "If they go for it, I'll be a-riding right along with them."

Sly stood up and started in to pacing the floor like as if he was real anxious for things to start in to hopping, but of course, we both knowed that we'd have another day and a half to wait it out. He turned on me right smart, and he said, "That's great work, Barjack. Great."

"The way I figger it," I said, "if you're a-waiting for them out there the way you done for that other one, you'll be in front of them and I'll be with them. Hell, I can drop back just a little and be behind them. We'll have their ass right where we want it."

"That's just how I'd have figured it, too," Sly said.

"Oh, yeah," I said, "they bragged on shooting you up the way they done. Never said nothing about me, though. They think they killed you."

"They'll learn better soon enough," he said, and his eyes just turned real cold. I was sure as hell glad the son of a bitch weren't after my ass. Well, I had me another few drinks, and then I went on to bed. The last thing I seen of ole Sly before I dropped off, he was still up and

pacing around. He was all tight strung and raring to go
a-killing.

I don't know if ole Sly got much sleep that night or
not, 'cause he was still a-sleeping whenever I got up the
next morning, and that was damned unusual. I tried to
keep quiet getting my ass dressed, but I went and
bumped my bare big toe on my left foot against the leg
of a chair, and the chair scooted and made a racket, and
I yowled out. I couldn't help myself. Sly come awake.

"You going out, Barjack?" he asked me.

"I figger I'd best hang out with them ole boys till
we're done with them," I said.

"That's a good idea," Sly said. "Keep me posted."

"I'll do my best," I said. I went ahead and got my
clothes on, strapped on my Merwin and Hulbert Company revolver, and then put the hat on my head. Then I
left the room and went on downstairs. I didn't see no
Jaspers, and I figgered they was all still a-sleeping it off
across the street, so I just went ahead and ordered me
up a breakfast of steak and eggs. It was pretty good, and
I washed it down with about a pot of coffee. 'Bout then
here come Orvel Jasper.

"Morning, Napoleon," he said.

"Pull up a chair, Pard," I said, and he did. He went
on ahead and ordered up his own breakfast, and then I
asked him, "Where's them brothers of yours?"

"Aw, hell," he said, "they're still sleeping it off. You
musta got up early, 'cause you're done finished with
your breakfast. Hell, Napoleon, you're still the drinking
champ around here. I got to hand it to you."

"Well," I said, "I had me a lot of practice. That's for
sure."

Me and ole Orvel set there together without saying much, and I could tell that he had something eating at his mind. I figgered I knowed what it was, too, but of course, I couldn't say nothing to him about it, 'cause I figgered that just maybe he was a-starting to worry about what it was that was taking his one brother so long in scouting out a place to rob that there stagecoach. I knowed that the son of a bitch was laying out there in the ditch where Sly had left him to rot, but like I said, I couldn't say nothing to Orvel about that, now could I?

He et his breakfast and drunk a bunch of coffee the same as what I had did, and by and by his two brothers come along. They was both of them a-moaning and holding their heads, and I wanted to laugh at them, but the mood Orvel was in, I figgered I maybe hadn't ought to do that. Pretty soon them other two had ordered them up some coffee and food, and it was while they was eating that Orvel final come out with it.

"Boys," he said, "I'm getting worried 'bout Oliver. Seems to me he'd oughta been back here by now."

"He has been gone awhile," Bud said. "You reckon something happened to him?"

"Aw, hell," Orren said, "Oliver can take keer a hisself."

"Maybe so," Orvel said, "but soon as you two finish up here, we're saddling our horses and going out to look for him."

"We find him out there and he's all right," Bud said, "he's going to sure as hell be mad at us. He told us right clear to wait for him here."

"Yeah, well, if that happens it'll sure relieve my mind," Orvel said, "and I'll take all the blame. Hurry it up, now." Then he looked over at me. "You wanta ride along with us, Napoleon?"

"Sure thing," I said.

Whenever they final got ready to leave, I told them I had to go out back to the outhouse and that I'd meet them down to the stables, so when they walked outa the place, I headed upstairs to tell Sly what we was a-doing. With all them Jaspers outa town at once like that, why, he'd be free to come down from the room again for a spell. I thought for a minute there that he might want to go on ahead and get the job over with, ride on out after us and catch them outa town like that, but he never said nothing about it, and so I let it go too. The only thing I could figger was that it come too fast, and he weren't ready. I went on down and on over to the stable.

Them Jaspers was all saddled up, and I got my own nag saddled as fast as I could. I knowed they was anxious to get a-moving. At least, ole Orvel was. We rid outa town in the direction of that stagecoach route. I recanized the way. 'Course, I couldn't let on that I knowed a damn thing about it. I knowed it was fixing to be a long ride out there, and so I had packed in a few bottles of good whiskey. I knowed, too, that once they was to find their brother's dead and stinking corpus out there where me and ole Sly had left it, they'd be a-needing a drink too. That's how come me to carry along a extry like I done.

For a while the youngest two, 'special that Bud, was talking all the time, but Orvel weren't in no mood for it, and after he'd told them to shut up several times, they final got the hint. We rid along quiet after that. When we had got way on down the road along about midafternoon, and we was damn near to the place where Sly had kilt that Jasper, Orvel got to looking real worried.

"There's plenty good spots right along here," he said. "He shoulda done picked one out and come on back to tell us."

We rid on, and we went right past that body. I kept quiet. I didn't let on nothing. I sure didn't want it being too obvious that it was easy for me to spot it. If the weather had been warmer than what it was, there wouldn'ta been no way we coulda rid past a corpus like that. There woulda been too much evidence in the air, but they never noticed a thing, and so I made out like I never either. We got on down the road a ways, and Orvel stopped us.

"The country's opening up too much," he said. "He wouldn'ta come way out here. We passed by all the good spots back yonder. Let's turn around and go back."

This time as we was riding through that part of the road what kinda had walls on each side, where the road was like a narrow little valley, and where in fact their dead brother was at, Orvel told us to go slow and look real careful for any kinda sign.

"Well, what're we looking for?" Bud asked him.

"Just shut up and look," Orvel said.

I knowed what he was a-thinking, and I figgered he didn't want to put it into so many words. And you know, I begun to actual feel some bad for them ole boys. They wasn't such bad boys after all. They was good drinking pardners, that's for sure, and ole Orvel 'special was sometimes a hell of a lot of fun. I had come to like him all right. But that don't mean I was softening up on the

notion of killing the sons of bitches for what they done
to me and ole Sly. No sir. Right is right.

Well, we come up on the place where the corpus was
at, and it looked to me like they was all a-going to ride
right on past it again, so I kinda eased my ole horse real
close over to the ditch on the right-hand side of the road,
and when I come up alongside of it, I stopped.

"Orvel," I said.

He stopped his horse and twisted in the saddle to look
over at me. His brothers stopped too. "What is it?" he
said.

I set there on my horse a-looking down into that there
ditch. "I sure hope I ain't found what we're a-looking
for," I said, and I pointed down at it. Orvel come riding
over quick-like, and he seen it right away. He jumped
down offa his horse's back and stepped right over to the
edge of the ditch. He stood there looking down for a few
seconds without saying nothing, and his brothers was
coming up to stand beside him.

"It's him," Orvel said. "That's Oliver."

"Somebody's kilt him," Bud said. "Who done it?"

"We might not never know," Orren said.

"Let's get him buried," said Orvel.

I helped them with that unpleasant task, and I really
got to feeling sorry for the poor bastards having to bury
their own brother like that, and him not in the best condition neither. You might think I'm lying, but I really
did feel for them. I had me some brothers once myself,
but whenever I run off from New York City when I was
just a kid, I left them behind and never seen nor heard
from any of them since then. I always figgered they
never missed me, 'cause there was way too many of us

back then anyhow, but I did sort of know what kinda feelings brothers has for each other.

Well, we put the stiff in a hole we dug, and then we covered it back up, and we all of us stood around the fresh grave with our hats in our hands and our chins on our chests. Bud sniffled some, and Orvel sudden looked up into the sky. "Oliver never deserved this what he got," he said. "I hope you let us come to know just who done it to him so we can get even. But right now, we're just going to go ahead with the plans he made for us. Wherever you got him up there, take keer of him for us, will you?" He put his hat back on then, so I figgered that the service was all did.

"I'm sure awful sorry about this, fellas," I said whenever we was walking back toward the horses. "What you said back there, Orvel, does that mean that we're going on ahead with the stagecoach job tomorry?"

"Hell, yes," said Orvel. "Oliver scouted it all out, and we're going through with it. He'd want it that way. He'd expect it of us."

"It's just only tomorrow afternoon," Orren said. "That don't hardly give us proper mourning time."

"We're going to be right here tomorrow afternoon," said Orvel. "I figger this here is the place that he picked out. I don't know who the hell come across him and kilt him here, but he meant for us to take that stagecoach right here, and we're going to do it. I don't want to hear no more talk about it."

Well, for sure that was the end of the discussion. I guess them boys was used to taking orders from the oldest, and with that Oliver gone, Orvel was it. He had inherited the boss's role, and the others just went and accepted it thataway. So I knowed then that me and Sly was going to get our chance that next day. I also knowed that some way, I was going to have to let Sly know about the details. I didn't think that would be too hard to do. I figgered we'd all just go back into town here in a bit and get to drinking again, and I'd just wait for them to pass out again, and then I'd go and see Sly. Thinking about drinking made me remember them two bottles I had brung along. I went and fetched one outa my saddlebags.

I tuck me a slug and offered it to Orvel. He tuck it without saying a word and had him a long drink. Then he passed it on to Orren, and Orren passed it on to Bud. Bud tuck his drink and handed it back to me, and we kept it going thataway till the damn thing was empty. "I got another one over here," I said. Pretty soon we was all drunk as skunks, and Orvel said that we was going to spend the night right there and wait for that damn stagecoach to show up tomorrow.

Chapter Eighteen

Well, I couldn't have that, and I reckon you know how come. Hell, I wouldn't have no way of getting my ass on back to ole Sly and letting him know just what the hell was fixing to happen or just where at. And if ole Sly never made it out there where we was at on time, why, I'd have me just only two choices to choose from. One was that I'd have to try to drop back and shoot all three of them bastards from behind, and I'd have to shoot them fast and accurate so that number three wouldn't have the time to turn on me. That didn't seem like such a good plan to me. I didn't like the odds a damn bit.

But if I was to choose not to try it, that only left me just one other thing to do, and that was that I'd have to go on ahead and really help the son's of bitches rob the goddamn stagecoach. Then what if they was to go and kill the driver or something like that? Which thing I figgered was a genuine and distinct possibility. Why, hell, I'd be a damned ax-sessory to the whole thing. Worse yet. What if the stage had it a shotgun rider what was ever' bit as good as ole Ash Face? Hell, he might blow some one of the outlaws away, and it might could just wind up to be me. Well, I didn't like neither one of the possibilities what seemed to be a-shaping up there. So I thought real hard about the situation.

"We're going to get awful hungry," I said, "before that stage comes around tomorry afternoon."

"I'm hungry already," Bud said.

I pulled out my ole Merwin and Hulbert Company self-extracting revolver and acted like as if I was a-checking it over to get it ready, and I said, "I ain't none too good with this thing here. If I'd knowed we was a-going to be staying out here all this time, hell, I'd a brung my shotgun along with me. I feel a lot better if I got my shotgun along. You know, I heard about a shotgun rider up north what blowed a bandit clean offa his horse and nearly blowed him in half with his shotgun. A damn six-gun ain't hardly no match for a shotgun. No, sir. But I reckon I'll just have to make do with what I got here. Hell, maybe they won't even put up no kind of argument when they see that there's four of us against them."

"My stomach's growling," Bud said.

I went over to my ole horse and pulled the last bottle we had drank out of back outa the saddlebag, and I tuck myself a good long drink. I already knowed there weren't enough in there to go around and give ever'one a decent suck on it, and I never let on that I had a couple of extries stashed away. When I lowered that bottle I smacked my lips real loud, and then I offered the bottle over to ole Orvel. He tuck it and had hisself a drink. He handed it to Orren, and Orren tuck a drink, and then there weren't nothing left. Bud said, "Hey." I had them other bottles in my other saddlebag, but I never let on. Orvel licked his lips like as if they was parched, and he was dying of thirst.

"Hell," he said, "let's go on back to town."

"Well now, Orvel," I said, "I guess I don't really need that damned ole shotgun."

"Come on," he said. "Let's go."

So we all mounted up and headed back the way we had come out. Nobody said nothing much on the ride back, and whenever we got into town, we all tied up there in front of the place where me and ole Sly was holed up at. We went on in there and ordered us up some steaks and stuff, and, of course, a bottle of whiskey. We got the whiskey and our glasses first, and ole Orvel poured us each a drink. I turned mine down right fast and got another one. I drunk it all down, and then I said, "I got to go out back."

I walked out the back door and right up the outside stairs what led up to the second floor. I found ole Sly in the room with a meal and a pot of coffee. He looked up and said, "I saw you riding in, so I got myself right back up here as fast as I could."

"Listen here," I said. "I got to get my ass on back down there and join back up with them assholes. We're a-fixing to rob the stage tomorry afternoon almost just right there where you kilt that other Jasper at. By the way, his first name was Oliver, if you keer about that sort of thing."

"What time will you be headed out in the morning?" he asked me.

"Orvel ain't said," I told him. "I'll try to let you know tonight."

"All right," he said. "Good luck to you."

I went back the way I had come, so that them Jaspers never seen me come down the stairs, and when I set back down with them, here come our steaks. We all et like we hadn't et in a week, and then we went to drinking more whiskey. I had to go to pretending again, 'cause I wasn't hardly feeling nothing but just good, and them other three boys was all starting in to getting woozy. Orvel poured another round of drinks, and the bottle was way down low. Ole Bud lurched up from his chair. "I'll get another one," he said, talking slurry-like.

He staggered on over to the bar, and he run into a cowboy what was standing there. The cowboy had been just about ready to tip up a beer glass for a drink, and whenever ole Bud knocked into him, he spilt that beer all down his shirtfront. "Goddamn it," he said. "Whyn't you watch where the hell you're going?"

Bud looked up at the other man, but the way he looked, I ain't at all sure he could see much of anything. "Well," he said, "why don't you just watch out for where I'm going, mister?" The cowboy tuck ahold of Bud's shirtfront and give him a hell of a shove, and ole Bud went flying back and fell over on his ass and scooted along the floor for a few feet. Orvel was up right-quick, looking mean as hell and facing that cowboy. I could see right away that Orvel was ready to draw on the man and shoot him dead. I had to act fast. I picked up our nearly empty whiskey bottle by its neck and stood up.

"Hey, cow's ass," Orvel said, "that's my little brother you throwed down on the floor."

"So what?" the cowhand said.

"I mean to kill you," said Orvel.

Just then I stepped up behind the cowboy and swung that bottle and bashed him in the back of the head. He dropped like a rock, and Orvel give me a mean look. "What the hell you do that for?" he said. "I was going to kill the son of a bitch."

"I was afraid you'd do just that," I said, "or else he'd kill you. I didn't want neither one of them things to happen."

"You didn't have no business interfering, Napoleon," Orvel said, and he turned on me, and he still had that same meanness in his eyes. He looked like as if he was a-fixing to draw down on me. I had spoilt his game with the cowboy, so he meant to just put me in that cowboy's place. You know damned well by now just how I feel about a face-to-face gunfight. I had to come up with something right-quick.

"Listen to me," I said, and I walked right on over close to him, "s'pose you'd killed the bastard. The law woulda come around to find out what happened here, and you mighta had to fight a lawman or two or else go set in the jailhouse for a spell. Or s'pose instead you went and got your own self kilt. Either way, it woulda really finished off our plans for tomorry afternoon, now wouldn't it? And what would ole Oliver think about all that? Let's get this little job all did, and then you can go on and get yourself in all the gunfights you want to. It won't make a damn to me then."

Well, he thought about that for a spell, at least that's what he looked like he was a-doing, and then I guess, drunk as he was, he seen the wisdom of my words. He walked back over to the table and set back down with me. I heaved a big sigh of relief. Orvel stayed kinda sulky, though, and he hollered out for a fresh bottle. Bud got hisself up offa the floor, and the barkeep put a bottle on the bar. Bud grabbed it and weaved his way back over to the table. Orvel jerked the bottle away from Bud and poured hisself a drink. He didn't bother pouring none for the rest of us.

I picked up the bottle then and poured the rest of the round. Bud finished that one off too fast, and he went and passed on out with his head down on the table. In two more rounds, Orren looked like as if he was about to go under. Orvel was still sulking, but he looked pretty close to gone too. Then he kinda brung hisself up out of it, and he give me a look.

"Let's get these two sissy brothers of mine on to bed," he said.

"Sure," I said. "Whenever we get that all did, I reckon I'll come back here and turn in myself. We going to get a early start in the morning, ain't we?"

"We'll get an early start, all right," Orvel said, giving me a real sly kinda look, "but you're staying over at our room. We're sticking together real close till this job's done tomorrow."

I started in to say I needed to go get my shotgun then, but it come to me that if he was meaning for us to stick together, he might just follow my ass up to the room, and there would be ole Sly a-setting there playing cards with hisself. I didn't want that to happen, so I kept quiet. Like we done the time before, I helped him to lug his damn sloppy-ass drunk brothers across the street and on up to their room, but first I stuck that nearly fresh bottle in my jacket pocket. Over in their room, there was them two beds, and we throwed them two on top of one of them. Orvel pointed to the other'n.

"You and me'll sleep there," he said. Damn, but I wanted to see ole Sly and tell him what was happening. He did know, though, that the robbery was planned for the next day in the afternoon, so maybe he'd figger something out. I sure did hope so. I didn't want to be out there alone with them three whenever that stage come rolling along. But there didn't seem to be nothing for it but for me to lay on down there alongside of ole Orvel and try to get me some shut-eye. So I did.

Them other two boys commenced to snoring and snorting something awful just about then, and I thought that I'd never get me no sleep. I kept a-trying, but it just didn't work out. Final, though, ole Orvel went on to sleep, and he snored louder'n them other two put together. I come up real easy outa that bed, and then I stood there for a bit to see if I had disturbed Orvel, but he never moved. He just kept on a-snoring. I slipped on my boots and my jacket and strapped my revolver back on. I hadn't tuck nothing else off. I put the hat on my head and tippy-toed outa the room, shutting the door behind me real easy-like.

The town was deader'n hell, and the night was cold. I crossed the street, went into the saloon and on upstairs to the hotel part of the place. Sly was still up and awake.

He was standing there at the winder, so I guessed he had saw me a-coming when I was crossing the street.

"Bastards final all went to sleep," I said. "Or passed out. Orvel said we had to all stick together till after the job tomorrow."

"Did you find out anything more?" Sly asked me.

"Just only that we're heading out early," I said. "I never got no specific time outa that son of a bitch."

"They all get pretty drunk then?" he said.

"I reckon," I said.

"So it might not be quite as early as they meant for it to be," he said.

"Well," I said, "likely you're right about that. And once they do all come around in the morning, if one of them don't say nothing first, I'm going to suggest that we have us a good breakfast before we take off to do meanness."

"That will give me plenty of time," said Sly. "I'll be up and out before sunup. I'll ride out there and find me a place to wait for them."

"Whenever you show yourself," I said, "I'll fall back some. We'll have them from both sides."

I thought that ole Sly might argue with me on that, 'cause that would put me where I could shoot them in the back, and he didn't care for that sort a thing, if you recall, but he never. He just said, "I'd better turn in then if I mean to be out before daylight. And you need to get back over there so they don't know you slipped out on them."

"If anyone notices and says anything," I told him, "I'll just say I had to go take a piss."

I found my shotgun and tuck it up, and then I left the

room. I went on back over to where the Jaspers was staying at and slipped back in. I propped my shotgun in a corner, tuck off my hat, my gunbelt, my jacket and my boots, and then I stepped over to the bed real quiet-like. I listened for a bit to them bastards all a-snoring, and then I laid my ass down there again beside ole Orvel. He snorted and rolled over, but that was all. I had made it all right.

But their damn snoring was making me crazy. I had images swimming in my head of the sun a-coming out and shining in through the winder and me still a-laying there wide awake and listening to that shit. That seemed like a downright dreary prospect. I slipped my ass up and outa the bed one more time and went to get that bottle outa my jacket pocket. I tuck it back to bed with me. After a few good pulls on that thing, I got myself drowsy enough to drop on off to sleep. That's just one more reason to give thanks to heaven for good whiskey.

Well, I had been up the longest and had drunk the most and the latest, but I was still the first one awake in the morning. I got my ass on up and got myself all pulled together, and I walked over to the winder to look out. I could see just a tiny bit of color on the far east horizon. I stood there for a minute or so, and then I seen ole Sly a-headed for the stable. I figgered I'd give him a good head start, and then I'd wake them damn Jaspers up. I went on ahead and checked my Merwin and Hulbert and my shotgun, making sure they was both good and ready for action. I found the bottle and had myself a wake-up snort of whiskey, and then I went and lit me up a good ceegar.

I set down and smoked that ceegar down a ways, and

then about half of that ole sun ball was a-showing out there, and the day was starting in to light up. I looked out the winder down onto the street again, and there was a few folks starting in to walk around out there. I went back over to the bed and give ole Orvel a shake. He come awake like as if he was ready for a fight.

"It's damn near daylight out there," I said. "You said you wanted us to get a early start."

He set up on the edge of the bed and rubbed his eyes with the back of his hands. Then he give a kick to the other bed. "Hey," he hollered. "Get your lazy asses up." Well, them other two didn't have to do nothing to get dressed, 'cause they hadn't never undressed. And all ole Orvel had to do was to just pull on his boots and strap on his six-gun. We headed out the door, but on the way, I picked up my shotgun. Orvel reached out a hand and tuck hold of my shoulder to stop me.

"Wait a minute," he said. "When did you get that damn thing?"

"What?" I said, real innocent-like.

"That damn shotgun," he said. "When did you get it?"

"Hell," I said, "I don't know what time it was. I had to get up and go out to the outhouse. So long as I was out anyhow, I stopped by my room for it."

"I told you," Orvel said, "we was sticking together till this job is done."

"I didn't figger you meant I was to piss in the bed," I said.

"Come on," he said, and he led the way out the door. Ole Orvel, he had really developed hisself a grouchy attitude for some reason. I told myself then that I was going to be double glad to see him deader'n a flat toad.

We follered him on out and over to the place across the street, where we ordered up coffee and breakfasts. None of them Jaspers said much of anything the whole time we was in there, and I was just as glad. They was all three some groggy from the night before, and they each groaned a bit now and then, so I think their heads was a-hurting them. That all seemed like good signs to me.

Well, we drunk us up about three pots a coffee and et our breakfasts, and I figgered ole Sly had a hell of a good head start on us by then, so I decided to try to get the day a-going. "It's getting late," I said. "Hadn't we ought to be getting a move on?"

"Shut up, Napoleon," Orvel said. "I'll tell you when it's time to go."

For someone what had started out telling me how much he liked me, Orvel had turned some surly, and I ain't sure just what turned him that away. 'Course, he had just buried his one brother, and I had talked us into coming back into town after he had said we'd stay out there on the damn prairie for the night. Maybe he just didn't like having his orders questioned, 'special if the one what was doing the questioning won out in the end. Anyhow, all I done was I just give a shrug, and I poured myself another cup of coffee. Well, that done it. Orvel shoved his chair back and stood up.

"Let's go," he said.

As we walked outa that place and down the street toward the stable, I seen that ole Bud was still a-staggering some. Hell, I thought, the little bastard is still drunk, and I believe he was, too. His two older brothers wasn't in much better shape, but I figgered they'd likely all be sober by the time we had made it all the way out to that sticking-up spot. 'Course, it'd be too late for them by that time, 'cause the by God Widdermaker would be there a-waiting for them, and I'd be dropping back behind them with my shotgun. Let them sober up, I said to myself, for all the good it'll do their asses.

We got our horses and got them saddled up and ready to go. I still had them two unopened bottles of whiskey in my saddlebag, but I never said nothing about it nor let on in no way, 'cause by then I was figgering that it would be my celebrating whiskey after them Jaspers was all dead. We rid outa town together, moving kinda slow and staying real quiet. No one had nothing to say, and there ain't no more for me to say about it till we got near all the way out there.

We was getting close to the spot whenever Orren pulled a watch outa his pocket. I wondered just what poor son of a bitch he had kilt in order to steal that thing offa the corpus. Anyhow, he looked at it real squinty eyed for a few seconds, and then he said, "We're getting here early, ain't we?"

" 'Course we are," Orvel said. "I meant for us to. We got to find ourself a good hidey hole to wait for that there stage coach. What I figger is, we'll put two of us, one on each side of the road, and then we'll do the same thing a little farther on back. Whenever that stage comes along, we'll let it get past the first two. Then the other two'll step out into the road and stop it. If the driver and the shotgun rider act like they mean to put up a fight, why then the other two'll step on out and holler at them from behind. That way, they'll be surrounded. You see?"

"That ought to work," I said.

"You damn right it'll work," Orvel snapped back at me.

I figgered then that it was a good thing this was a one-time deal, and them Jaspers was all fixing to get killed, 'cause I couldn't see no way that I'd be able to get along with ole Orvel for even just one more day if I'da had to. I was ready to kill that bastard right then and there, but of course, I knowed that I'd better wait it out a little longer. It give me some pleasure thinking about what they had coming, too, I can tell you that, and what's more, I ain't ashamed to admit it neither.

We rid on down the road a little more farther, with Orvel a-studying the sides and a-looking for suitable hidey-holes. I looked over at Bud, and he still looked like what he really wanted was he really wanted to be laying down somewhere rather than be laying in for a stagecoach. Orren was in a little better shape than what Bud was, but I sure didn't figger this bunch was going to give me and ole Sly no trouble. Then I got to thinking about the actual killing what was a-coming up.

The way I woulda liked to have done it woulda been if ole Sly would show hisself the way he done to Oliver, and while the bastards was startled from the sight of the man they thought they had done kilt, I would drop back just a bit and blast at least one ass with my shotgun. I might even be able to get two of them. It would be a real easy thing for ole Sly, good as he was, to gun the other one or two from the front the way he liked to do it. I thought about that awhile, but only there was just one thing I didn't really like about it. Something in me wanted each one of the sons of bitches to know who I was and how come I was killing them.

Chapter Nineteen

Orvel, he stopped of a sudden, and he got him a look on his face like as if he had just come up with the most brilliantest idee anyone in the whole entire history of the world had ever come up with. He didn't say nothing at all for a spell, nary a word, just set there a-studying on the road and the sides of the road, squinnying his eyeballs around and looking real proud of hisself. Final, ole Bud, who had the least patience of the whole bunch of us gethered there, just couldn't take it no more. He spoke up and said, "What is it, Orvel?"

"Shut up," Orvel said. "I'm thinking. Can't you see that?" Then, "Napoleon," he said, "you see that big rock up yonder on the ridge?"

"I see it," I said, and of course, there weren't no way coulda not saw it 'cept only if I'd been a blind man, but I didn't tell Orvel that. You see, we was on the road where it dropped way on down, and the ground on each side of the road riz up high, and so there was a high ridge on each side of the road there. We was also at a place where the road tuck a sharp curve. So the stage, what would already be a-climbing up the hill, would have to slow down even more to make that curve, and the driver and the guard wouldn't be able to see who or what might be a-waiting around the curve there for them. I could see all that right away. It didn't take no brilliant brain to figger all that out.

"I want you to get your ass up there," Orvel said, "and hide yourself on back behind that there rock."

"All right," I said. I started to turn my horse around to go and find me a way up to the top, but he stopped me.

"Wait up," he said. Then he looked over at his little brother Bud. "Bud," he said, "I want you to go on the other side of the road and get up there just direct across from ole Napoleon. You got that?"

"But I ain't got me no rock over there," Bud said with a kinda whimper in his little sissy voice.

"Never mind that," Orvel said. "Just get up there like I said and lay low. Now, listen here, both of you. Put your horses back outa sight, and whenever that stage comes a-rolling in here, don't let them see you up there. Keep hid. Just let it roll right on past you. You hear me?"

"I got you," I said.

"Yeah," said Bud. "Let it go by. Okay."

"Me and Orren," Orvel said, "we'll be just down here on the road, and just when the stage comes around the curve moving real slow like it'll be doing, we'll step out into the road and stop them. That's when you two stand up and show yourselfs. They'll see the two of us right in front of them down on the ground there, and the two of you behind them up on the hillsides. Understand?"

"Seems easy enough to me," I said. "That oughta buffalo them real good. We might not even have to shoot no one."

I hoped that there last little remark of mine might soak into ole Orvel's head and let him know that there weren't no need to do no killing. A course, that was all just in case ole Sly didn't show up there before the stagecoach, and I was to have to go and help them bastards in the robbing of it.

"All right," Orvel said. "Go on."

Me and ole Bud rid down the road together for a ways till we come on a place where we could each of us get off the road on our own opposite sides, then double back and get our ass up onto them ridges where Orvel had told us to be. All this time I was a-wondering just where in hell ole Sly could be hid out at. I wondered how far off he had hid his horse so we wouldn't see it. It come on me then that the son of a bitch might not even be nowhere near, and I had me just a mite of panic set in just then. Them two choices I had run over in my mind earlier come back to me, and I knowed that if it come to that, I wouldn't know which way I was going to go till I'd done went.

I turned my horse to go off on the south side of the road, and Bud, he went the other direction. "I'll wave at you when I get up there," he said. I told him okay and rid on. I kept on a-looking for any sign that Sly was anywhere close by, but I never seen none. I was getting some nervous about the whole thing, I can tell you. Well, pretty damn soon, I found myself back at that boulder what Orvel called a big rock, and so I tuck my horse back away from the road a ways so no one would see him up on the ridge, and I left him there. I tuck my rifle and my shotgun with me, and of course I had my Merwin and Hulbert revolver strapped on, and I walked on over to that boulder. I had me a hell of a view from up there of the road in both directions.

Whenever I got myself over there in place, I stood up real clear and waved down to ole Orvel so he'd know I was where I was s'posed to be at. Just then Bud showed his ass over on the opposite ridge, and he give me a wave, and I waved back at him. Then I ducked back behind that boulder and found me a way I could snuggle down where I could watch the road but not be saw by anyone down there. I hadn't saw nor heard nothing of the stage, and I figgered we'd have us a pretty good wait, so I wanted to get my ass real comfortable.

I tuck me out a ceegar and lit it, knowing full well that it might piss off ole Orvel if he was to catch sight of my smoke a-billowing up from behind that big rock, but I figgered there was plenty of time. I could see way down the road, and so I'd see the stagecoach a-coming way before they'd notice my ceegar smoke. Then I could put it out and wait for them. I figgered if Orvel was to yell at me, I'd tell him that, but Orvel never said nothing. Likely he never even noticed nothing.

Then I heard the slow and easy clopping of a horse riding in casual-like from the west. That was the same direction the stage would be coming in from later. I scooted around for a good look, and by God, it was the ole Widdermaker hisself a-coming on in for the kill. My heart commenced to pounding real hard in my chest. Bud raised up his head and looked over at me, and I waved him back down. He was stupid enough to mind me. Sly come riding on in. I wondered if he knowed where we all was at or was he riding right smack into the ambush what had been set up for the stagecoach. I decided I couldn't take no chance. I stood up.

"Sly," I yelled out, and he looked up and seen me and stopped his horse. "There's one direct across from me," I called out, "and there's two more just around the curve a-hiding out."

He stepped down offa his horse, turned it around, and give it a slap on the ass. It trotted back west a ways and stopped. Then he just stood there right smack in the middle of the road alone. "Jaspers," he called out. "Show yourselves." I looked back east and down on the road, and I seen ole Orvel starting in to kinda sneak outa his hidey-hole off the side of the road. "Who's that?" he hollered. The Widdermaker answered, "Herman Sly."

Orvel stepped on out, still somewhat tentative-like, though. "You ain't no Herman Sly," he yelled. "Sly's dead. We killed him deader'n hell. Who are you? What's this all about?"

"Come out and take a look for yourself," Sly said. "I won't shoot. At least I won't shoot first."

Orvel walked on out to the middle of the road and started in real slow to walking around the curve. He was a-craning his neck, poking his head out in front of the rest of him like as if he was trying to peek around a corner. He waved a arm back behind hisself. "Come on, Orren," he said, and I seen Orren come out and foller along. Each one of them boys had a six-gun already in his hand. Then, across the road on top of the other ridge, I seen Bud stand up kinda slow-like. He seen his brothers, and he pulled out his own revolver. I knowed what ole Sly was up to, but I also thought he was plumb crazy. I mean, there was them two down below on the same level what he was on, and then there was that other'n up above him just across the road from me, and they all done had their irons in their paws, and there was Sly with both of his Colts still in the holsters, and I knowed that he meant to let the damn Jaspers shoot first. That was his style.

You know, it's one thing to know all about a feller's reputation and to even have saw him in action and to know that he's just about the fastest and most deadliest son of a bitch on the face of the whole entire world and to even believe in him one hundred percent, but it's a whole 'nother thing to be partnered up with him and a-waiting for a big shoot-out like that. I was skeered to death clean down to my dirty socks that he was a-fixing to stop a bullet the way he was a-doing.

Orvel and Orren come on around the curve, still moving catlike, and they stopped still when they seen ole Sly a-standing there. His Colts was still both holstered. They didn't say nothing at first. I reckon they was plumb astonished at the sight of him just a-standing there. Just like their dead brother, they thought for sure they had kilt him. That had to of set them back some, and then the sight of him just a-standing there without even a gun in his hand like he weren't skeered of nothing in the universe, not God nor the Devil, was a mite unsettling too.

"Goddamn it," Orvel said. "Sly? It really is you. We all thought you was dead."

"It's me, all right," Sly said. "Alive and well, and I've come to kill you."

"Was it you, then, what killed Oliver?" Orvel asked him.

"I did that," Sly said, "with pleasure, and I'm here to kill the rest of you."

"Him and me both," I hollered. Like I said, I wanted to make sure they knowed who the hell I was and how come me to be a-gunning for them as well as the Widdermaker. "My name's Barjack. I ain't no goddamned Napoleon, and I was the one a-standing right next to Sly there when you went and shot us damn near to pieces, you chicken sons of bitches."

"You're Barjack?" Orvel said.

"I done said it," I told him. "I'm Barjack."

"I heard about you, Barjack," Orvel said. "I ain't got nothing against you. Shooting you was a accident. You was just in the way. We didn't even know who you was."

"You like to killed me just the same," I said.

"There's been enough talk," Sly said. "Get to shooting. That's what we're here for."

"I don't know, Sly," Orvel said. "I heard you never shoot first. What if we just turn around and walk away from you?"

"I'll make an exception in your case," Sly said. "Now, shoot."

Now, I think I done told you that ole Bud, what was the youngest of them bastards, was also the one without no patience to speak of, and I guess Bud's patience, what little he had, was done worn out by then. Likely he got nervous, too, knowing that there was two men there to kill him and his brothers, and one of them was the Widdermaker what they thought was dead, and the other'n was Barjack what had been writ about in Dingle's dime novels. Anyhow, it was just then that I seen ole Bud raise up his six-gun and take aim at Sly. I didn't have time to do much thinking.

"Look out, Sly," I yelled out, and I raised my rifle and snapped off a shot at Bud. I missed him, though, I'm ashamed to say, but it throwed his shot off, too, and it give Sly time to draw and whirl and send a slug right up there into Bud's chest. Bud fell over frontwards and fell clean down into the road and landed with a thud. Orren and Orvel both started in to shooting then, but they was a little far away from either Sly or me for good six-shooting, and their shots was going wild. I raised up my rifle again and tuck aim at the back of Orren, but the son of a bitch missed fire on me. I cussed and throwed it down into the road and picked up my shotgun and blasted both barrels down kinda between them two. I guess some of the shot skittered around and peppered them both some, but it didn't do no real damage. It did make them both yelp and hop around and dance some and tuck their attention offa Sly for just a bit. He pointed his Colt and brought down Orren right-quick.

Orvel, he turned and run back toward where his horse was hid, and his running tuck him outa even Sly's revolver range. My rifle was down in the road, and my shotgun was empty. I knowed that I wouldn't be able to drop ole Orvel with just only my ole Merwin and Hulbert, and I don't know what the hell come over me, but

Orvel was down there below me a-running, and before I knowed what the hell I was a-doing, I had bent my knees to give me some spring, and I pushed with them as hard as I could, and I jumped straight up into the air. I went a-flying. By God, I flapped my wings and soared. I went a-sailing out over the road, and down below I could see Sly a-looking up at me, and I could see Orvel running like hell for his horse.

I could feel that cold air on me as I sailed with the wind, and then I kinda tilted my arms and shoulders and tuck me a deliberate turn, and I headed myself right for Orvel. I come at him like a chicken hawk a-diving at a chicken, and he looked back over his shoulder, still a-running, and he looked right at me. He seen me swooping right down at him, and he turned to brace hisself for the impact, and he tried to raise up his six-gun, but he weren't near fast enough for my Ickrus act. I smashed into him something fierce. The top of my head rammed him right in the face, and I reckon I knocked out all of his front teeth and broke his nose and maybe at least one jawbone.

He went down hard flat on his back, and I crashed down right on top of him. I was all right, my landing having been cushioned pretty good by Orvel. I rolled offa him, and he was a-making all kinds of funny noises laying there on the ground and flailing his arms around some. Whenever I crashed into him, he had lost his grip on his six-gun, and it was laying off at a safe distance. I stood up and brushed myself off, and Sly come a-trotting up to stand there beside me.

"Barjack, that was amazing," he said.

"Yeah," I said, "well, it weren't the first time, as you well know."

He looked down at the messy face of Orvel Jasper. "I guess we'll have to take this one into the sheriff," he said. "The other two are dead."

I heard the stagecoach rumbles in the road then, and I guess Sly did too.

"What do we do about that?" I said. "Stage is a-coming."

"We'll wait for it and tell the driver what happened here," he said, "as well as what their plans had been."

"Whyn't you go talk to them," I said. "You're a slicker talker than me."

He give a shrug. "All right," he said. "I don't mind."

I let him turn around and start in to walking west to meet the stage, and then I slipped my Merwin and Hulbert outa the holster. I cocked it and lifted it up some, and I seen, even through the mess what I had made of his face, ole Orvel open his eyes wide and look horrified.

"You shot me and ole Sly damn near to pieces," I said, "you son of a bitch," and then I pulled the trigger.

Well, a few wires around to the places where them Jaspers had done killings and such and a look through the dodgers there in the sheriff's office, as well as me being a fairly well-knowed lawman myself, and things was all cleared up with the local law regarding the demise of the notorious Jasper brothers. Me and Sly went on ahead and spent one more night there in our hotel room, had us a good supper that night, and I got drunk as hell by way of celebrating our victory. Ole Sly even tipped a few with me. We got us a good breakfast in the morning, too, so we was pretty well fortified for our long ride home. We packed up the next morning and headed back north, toward Asininity.

A course, we was closer on into the winter time of the year, and this time we was headed north and northeast, so we knowed we'd be moving into colder air the whole way, maybe even more goddamn snow. I kept a-waiting for ole Sly to jump me out about the way I had gone and finished off ole Orvel, but he never said nothing about it one way or the other. He did talk about my second flying act ever' now and then, though, and he made out each time like he had enjoyed it right well. We did run into some snow, but it never slowed us down too much. And each time we come to a town, we stopped for a good supper, a good night's sleep, and a good breakfast.

We spent several cold nights on the trail, though. Whenever we come back into the little town of Dog Creek, we looked up ole Constable Thurmond, 'cause, as you might recall, we had made him a promise to do that if we was still alive to do it. He was real glad to see us, and it could be that he was more than a little bit surprised, too.

"Did you catch up with them Jaspers?" he asked us.

"We did," said Sly.

"And what happened?" Thurmond asked.

"They won't be a-bothering no one else," I said. "Not never."

Thurmond, he got all excited. He told ever'one he seen that me and Sly had got the Jaspers, and him and some other town folks bought us the biggest and best supper they could find in that little dog-ass town. They also paid for all the whiskey I could drink. Sly didn't drink much. They put us up in a room for the night, and then damned if they didn't go and buy our breakfast in the morning. We thanked them kindly and then said our so longs to them fine folks and moved on out. Two nights later it snowed like hell on us, and that sure cut some time offa our return back home. But we made it eventual, and I was gladder to see Asininity than I had ever been before in my life.

When we rid on into town, the sun was already down. It was a cold night, so there weren't no one in the street, but then I seen Lillian step outa the White Owl and start in to lock the door. I give Sly a look. "Likely she needs someone to walk her home on a cold night like this here," I said. He smiled at me and rid on over there, and I hauled my ass up to the hitching rail in front of the Hooch House. I didn't know till just then how much I had missed the damn place. I got down outa the saddle and lapped the reins around the rail. Then I ducked under the rail a-groaning and straightened myself up kinda slow. I thought, I'm getting too old for this kinda crap. I walked on in, and Bonnie seen me right away.

"Barjack," she yelled out at the top of her voice, and you know, it has a high top. Then a bunch of others joined in the yelling and welcoming home. I was mobbed and slapped on the back till I damn near fell over. Final I shoved my way on through the crowd, moving toward my favorite table.

"Let me set down," I said, and they did. Good ole Aubrey was right there with my bottle and my tumbler. Bonnie plopped her ample ass down in the chair right next to me, scooched it over close, and grabbed onto my arm, and like to squoze the blood pressure out of it. She slobbered kisses all over the side of my face. Happy come over and set across from me and looked me right in the eyes with a big wide grin spread all across his silly face. Someone standing somewhere back behind me said, "Barjack, we thought we'd never see you again."

"I knowed you'd be back, Barjack," Bonnie said.

"Hell, yes, sweets," I said. "You know I can't stay away from you."

"Where's ole Sly?" Happy said. "Is he all right?"

"He's just fine," I said. "Right about now he's likely kissing my ex-wife good night over there at her front door what used to be my front door."

"Is he really going to marry up with Lillian and settle down right here in Asininity?" Bonnie asked me.

"He damn sure is," I said. "Leastways, that's what he told me."

"What about the Jaspers?" Happy said.

"There ain't no more Jaspers," I said.

"You got them?" Happy asked. "You get them all?"

"I didn't get them all," I said. "The Widdermaker accounted for some of them. Well, actual, the way it all happened, I shot just only one of them. Sly gets most of the credit. He kilt the other three hisself. I tell you boys what. You too, Bonnie, darling. That man deserves that widdermaking name he's got. I ain't never saw such a killing man. Why, he's shooting that damn Colt even before you seen that he reached for it."

"Damn," Happy said. "I wish I coulda saw him in action like that."

I tuck me a big gulp of my whiskey then, and I put the glass down and reached a ceegar outa my pocket.

Ole Bonnie tuck the match outa my hand and scratched it on the table and held the fire to the end a my ceegar for me. I puffed on it till I had it going good. Then I tuck me another drink.

"Yes sir," I said, "you ain't never seen nothing till you've saw ole Sly in action with them Colts of his."

Then I heard Sly. He had slipped right up behind me. "You're much too modest, Marshal," he said.

I looked over my shoulder, and there he was. "Come on and set with us," I said, and he did. I offered him a drink, and he surprised me all to hell by accepting it. "Is the wedding day all set up?" I asked him.

"Yes, it is," he said, and he smiled on that. "I hope you'll be there."

"Hell," I said, "this is one hitching-up that I wouldn't miss for nothing in this whole entire world."

"What do you mean he's too modest?" Bonnie said.

"Why, it was Barjack that got the last and the meanest of the Jaspers," Sly said, "and in order to do it, he had to fly again. He was magnificent."